A DOG CALLED LUCKY TIDE

**Look for these and
other APPLE PAPERBACKS
in your local bookstore!**

The Secret Life of Dilly McBean
by Dorothy Haas

The Lemonade Trick
by Scott Corbett

The Hidden Treasure
by John Rowe Townsend

Swimmer
by Harriet May Savitz

Short Season
by Scott Eller

The Mall from Outer Space
by Todd Strasser

A DOG CALLED LUCKY TIDE

William Koehler

AN
APPLE
PAPERBACK

SCHOLASTIC INC.
New York Toronto London Auckland Sydney

ISBN 0–590–41710–X

Copyright © 1988 by William R. Koehler. All rights reserved. Published by Scholastic Inc. APPLE PAPERBACKS is a registered trademark of Scholastic Inc.

12 11 10 9 8 7 6 5 4 3 2 1   8 9/8 0 1 2 3/9

Printed in the U.S.A.   11

First Scholastic printing, September 1988

To Lillian

A DOG CALLED LUCKY TIDE

1

Tim Bradley seemed not to hear the order of the *Cormorant*'s first mate. He stared intently across the boat's port rail.

"I told you to get down there and level off that ice!" The mate's huge fingers ground into Tim's shoulder. "Do I have to lead you?"

A man busy at the *Cormorant*'s wheel turned angrily toward the big man. "Lay off the boy, Joost. He's only sixteen, and he does more work than any of us. He'll have the ice ready for your fish."

Joost turned his small eyes to the man. "Shut up, Mower. He came whinin' to the captain about needin' a man's wages to pay his dad's doctor bills. I'm gonna see that he does a man's work. As for you — do your own job. It'll be money out of all our pockets if we don't get to the best fishin' first." He nodded over his shoulder. "Look."

The bow of another boat was knifing the water a scant twenty yards astern, holding just to the starboard of the *Cormorant*'s wake. Two other vessels were also pressing hard. Far behind, the fishing village of St. Helene resembled a group of toy buildings on the rugged Newfoundland coast. Those closest to the sea were a weathered gray; the paint was much whiter on those that dotted the grasslands which sloped from the coast to the timber high above the town.

Each man of the three crews was straining to over-take the *Cormorant*. The spray-drenched skippers leaned forward on their bridges as they read the colors of the water for short cuts across the reefs. The mates of the other boats could be heard coaxing their men to get the most out of the diesel engines, but none of their voices matched the threatening tones of Joost.

Joost turned back to see Tim still staring across the water. "Are you deaf?" he screamed.

Tim spoke without turning his head. "There's something moving in circles near the end of that reef. It's alive. It's a dog."

Joost's fingers ground deeper into the shoulder. "He can swim."

"He's caught. He needs help."

"Move!" The mate shoved Tim toward the icing hatch.

Well-muscled and wiry as he was, Tim's feet could only slide stubbornly across the deck as he braced against the mate's tremendous strength.

"Let go, Joost! I'll try to save that dog." A moment later, Tim flexed like a coiled spring and drove his left elbow into Joost's middle. As the mate doubled over, Tim slipped off his shoes. Joost rushed wildly at him, but Tim escaped his path by diving cleanly over the port rail.

"Man overboard!" the man at the wheel cried.

The captain whirled around on the bridge when he heard the shout, and his eyes followed in the direction of a pointing finger.

Tim swam steadily through the green water; by the time the *Cormorant* had put around, he was close enough to see that the dog, though still struggling weakly, could not move forward. As he closed in on the last few yards of the gap, the dog's big head turned toward him. Tim saw that a line was tied around the dog's neck that extended down into the water toward the shadow of a reef. He pulled closer to the dog and caught the knot so that he could keep the animal's steadily paddling forefeet away from him. While treading water, Tim ran his right hand down the rope as far as possible and jerked experimentally in all directions. The rope came up solid with each jerk. Tim started picking at the knot with the cold fingers of both hands. Though part of Tim's weight was hung on the dog, the big Newfoundland kept up his steady rhythmic paddling and made no effort to climb onto his rescuer. Finally the knot was loosened enough for Tim to open the noose and slide it over the dog's head.

Tim turned from the dog to the *Cormorant,* which was standing by, twenty feet from the threat of the shadowy reef. Mower, the second mate, whirled a line with a loop around his head and dropped it into the water near Tim's ready hand. Tim worked the rope over the dog's head, past his weakly pumping legs, and drew it tight.

Mower's pull on the line brought Tim and the dog close to the boat's side. Tim used the lift of a wave to heave himself up to where he could grasp Mower's outstretched hand. On deck, he joined the smiling second mate in pulling the Newfoundland aboard. Joost, on an order from the captain, stood back from the rail.

"Boy, he's a big one," Mower said. "If the meat wasn't wore off of him, we'd have had a time lifting him. Look — he's too weak to shake. Wonder how he got in that jam?"

The huge dog slumped weakly to the deck. It seemed that the last of his strength went into turning his eyes gratefully toward Tim and stirring his tail in the puddle that his draining coat was making around him. Tim reached over and patted the dog. "You're going to make it all right."

"Fall to it!" Joost yelled at the curious crew. "Figurin' what he's cost you, your bellies should be full of that dog." He glowered at Tim. "And full of that nosy kid. We're puttin' back to replace him with a man." He turned to the captain. "I guess you'll be wantin' a full crew, and either he goes or I go."

Tim's lean face set in hard lines beneath his mop of red hair. His green eyes narrowed as he looked up at Joost. "You ought to be shipping on a cattle boat, Joost — with the rest of the bulls."

With outstretched hands, the giant mate lunged toward Tim. His big foot hit a spot that was wet from the dog's dripping coat, though, and Joost thudded heavily onto his side.

Tim stood balanced, ready to move in any direction. "You ought to be more careful, Bull, where you put those big hooves," he taunted.

Joost came off the deck with a roar, then stood shaking in anger as the captain grabbed his arm.

Captain Nichols' look moved from the dog and held for several moments on Tim's tired face. He nodded toward the other vessels, now showing their sterns well to the seaward. "There's not much else we can do but put back. It wouldn't be good for the rest of us the way things stand between you and Mr. Joost."

"I just can't afford to lose this job, Captain," Tim said.

When the *Cormorant*'s skipper turned away and gave the orders that brought the vessel around, Tim's attention came to rest resentfully on the dog. By the time the *Cormorant* was sliding between the two great rocks that marked the mouth of St. Helene's harbor, the dog had gained strength. He raised to a sitting position and looked about with understanding in his dark eyes, as the slowly turning engines eased the vessel around the rocky shoulder that made the harbor a sanctuary against storms from all directions.

The *Cormorant* moved slowly along the gray face of a stone wall that rose straight up from the green water. A bell rang, and the vessel rumbled and shuddered as her screw reversed. She eased up to a wharf of planks that were twisted by years of moisture and sun. Though the wharf was against the rock wall on one side and overhung the water on the other, it was no more than twice the width of the *Cormorant*.

Its length would give rail space to eight or ten fishing boats, more than was needed for St. Helene's small fleet. From the edge of the wharf, barnacle-encrusted piles reached down through the quiet water for standing room on the rocky bottom. Farther back, shorter piles ran down from the wharf's beams to the solid base rock a few feet below the surface. The *Cormorant*'s engines held her against the wharf while her lines were made fast.

The captain turned to Tim. "By Friday, I'll have a closing check in your post office box."

Tim nodded his thanks. "I've only been on the job three days, but we can use whatever I get." For several moments, his green eyes blazed in contempt at the scowling mate; then he looked around at the other members of the crew. "Sorry I cost you all money. But I guess I'd do the same thing again."

The big dog watched Tim leave the boat. He got unsteadily to his feet and wobbled toward the rail. With a lunging jump that showed more determination than strength, he went over the *Cormorant*'s rail and slumped down weakly on the rough planks of the wharf.

Tim looked apologetically at the dog. "I guess I could have helped you ashore. But you made it over the rail, so you ought to be in shape to start mooching around town for handouts in an hour or so." Tim's face tightened as he continued to look at the dog. "You've cost me plenty in the last hour. A job, and a chance to hang onto our timberland. Well, anyway, you'll find your way home, or a place to hang out in town. You won't be causing me any more grief."

Tim turned from the dog and started up the stairway which ran like a passageway between two fish-conveyor belts, through a cut in the cliff, and up to St. Helene's main street. The town, smelling strongly of fish and the sea, was quiet except for the sounds that came from the fish cannery buildings which spread from the conveyors to the corners of the block-long business street. The town hall and a group of small offices shared the opposite side of the street with a large general store.

Wet clothes are not unusual in a fishing town, and Tim walked the length of the block, passing several acquaintances, without a question being asked. The block of pavement ended, and a narrow gravel road began which followed the edge of the bluff to the north of the town. Tim was a quarter of a mile down the road when he heard sounds on the gravel behind him. He looked back and froze in surprise. The big Newfoundland was plodding toward him with a mechanical weariness. He came up to nudge Tim's leg with the side of his muzzle. His tail, now nearly dry, swung with a slow, confident measure.

Tim's frown couldn't hide his admiration. "Boy, you must have a rubber constitution. I'd have bet you couldn't get up those wharf steps for an hour. But you made it and tracked me out here. Maybe if you knew the bad luck you brought me, you wouldn't have followed me." Tim's frown lightened. "I'll take you someplace where you won't be around to jinx me, but first I need to get into some dry clothes."

Tim's wet pants rustled softly in the chilly fall air as he resumed his walk down the road. Two miles from town, he turned into a lane that led back to a house and barn and henhouse that stood in a grove of spruce trees.

Tim's mother was coming from the henhouse with a basket of eggs as he rounded the rear corner of their house. He grinned as she looked curiously at the huge dog, and Tim's wet clothes.

"I had to fish him out of the water, and now he figures I'm his friend for life. But so far he hasn't been much of a friend to me. Anyone looking around town for him will hear I pulled him out of the water and keep looking till they find him. I was partway home before I knew he was following me. After I get some dry clothes and something to eat, I'll take him back to town. He'll probably drift away before I finish eating, though."

"I'll fix lunch while you change clothes."

As Tim followed his mother into the house, the dog was close behind. Tim eased the door gently shut against the black muzzle. "You'll be more apt to start heading home if I don't take you in and feed you."

Tim's mother had lunch on the table by the time he had changed into another pair of jeans and a light woolen shirt. While Tim was eating a big bowl of warmed-over stew and a dish of applesauce and cream, his mother worked at sprinkling clothes to be ironed. While he ate, he mulled over the best way to tell her what was on his mind.

"I got us into a bad situation, Mom," he began.

Slowly, in a worried tone, Tim told his mother about the dog's rescue and his trouble with the *Cormorant*'s first mate. When he finished, he looked with concern at the peculiar expression on Mrs. Bradley's face. "I can't tell what you're thinking, Mom. I thought you'd feel I did the right thing when I went after the dog."

"It was the right thing. I'm proud of you and your father will be proud when he hears about it. But your temper scares me. After all, Mr. Joost was the mate. And he's like a big wounded bear; he doesn't forget. I'm afraid your hotheadedness has gotten you into trouble."

Tim got up from the table and walked over to a topographical map that was pasted to the wall above an old-fashioned cupboard. He put a finger on the line which marked a small peninsula six miles north of St. Helene. "After Dad got hurt, my fishing job seemed to be our last chance of paying off the balance on our timberland." He turned to his mother with a reassuring smile. "But somehow there'll be a way. I'll find one.

Then when Dad's back in shape, and everything's squared away, I'll go back and finish school."

A slight sound drew Tim's attention to the kitchen's side window. The Newfoundland's front feet were resting on the sill, and his nose was tight against the glass as he moved his eyes about to locate the source of the voices.

"Mom," Tim said.

"Yes — I'll fix something for him to eat. I'll soak some dry bread in the rest of this stew."

In a few minutes, with his mother close behind him, Tim took a gray granite pan of food out to the dog. The Newfoundland, with the restraint of his breed curbing the eagerness of his hunger, met them at the back step.

Tim set the pan on the ground. "Here you are, Buddy."

The dog's dignity held until he had taken his first bite of the savory food, then the hunger in his big, gaunt frame took over. His head and neck jerked as he gulped the food down. Several times he broke the rhythm of his gulping and swallowing to look appreciatively at Tim and emphasize his gratitude with a sweep of his tail.

Tears came to Mrs. Bradley's eyes. "He must have been in the water a long time to work so much weight off that huge frame. We'll find another meal for him in a few hours."

11

The empty pan began to slide around under the pushing of the dog's tongue.

"He likes your cooking, Mom. If he lives on Newfoundland, that meal ought to give him strength enough to get started home. After that swim that cost me my job, I'll be scraping to bring in groceries for ourselves, without satisfying his appetite." Tim grinned cheerfully at his mother. "Not to mention paying off our timberland."

Mrs. Bradley looked at the gratitude on the dog's face. "Well, I'm awfully glad we had something to give you this time," she told the dog. "It would help some to know where you came from and what your name is."

"I've got an idea of what it should be," Tim said. "He reminds me of the tide when he moves around in that rolling, determined way. An unlucky tide, from the trouble he brought. Hey, Tide," he called, "where do you live?"

The dog's rolling gait brought him across the yard to Tim's side. His tail swung with easy confidence as he shoved the side of his head against Tim's leg. Tim gave the dog a pat, then picked up the feed pan and rinsed and filled it while he worked the clanking pump with his other hand. He set the water down for the dog, and with a thoughtful look on his face he followed his mother back into the kitchen and went again to the map on the wall.

Once more, Tim placed a finger on the shoulder of land that jutted out into the sea about six miles above St. Helene. His finger traced a reef that extended from the end of the peninsula straight out to sea for two miles. The peninsula then curved gracefully back until its lower end closed to within a few hundred feet of shore, a mere one-half mile above Tim's house. By its angle out to sea and its curve back toward shore, the hook formed a bay which was closed tightly from the open sea along its top and side, and opened by the channel between its narrow southern end and the mainland.

Tim punched the map with his finger and turned to his mother. "If there was a way we could start getting pulpwood down to the mill, we could make our payments and stay even with things until Dad is able to help again."

"Your father thought that he could cut and yard enough pulpwood so that the bank would be willing to give him a loan to pay for trucking it down to the mill," Mrs. Bradley said. "Probably they would have. But there's no use thinking about that now."

Tim's face set in hard lines as he stared down at the floor. "He'd've made it, too, if it hadn't been for the accident. Dad would never have been standing in the wrong place when the stack of logs rolled, if he hadn't been dull from doing two men's work. And there I was — sitting in school while he dragged himself into the dinghy and made it back to St. Helene. And all with a broken leg."

"Hush now," Mrs. Bradley said. "You've done everything you could. You got that fishing job within two days after the accident happened."

Tim made a wry face toward the window. "And lost it three days after I started, thanks to that dog. Now I'm out of school *and* a job." Suddenly he stopped, and looked sharply at his mother. "Mom, I'm going up to our timber."

Mrs. Bradley shook her head. "No. It was too much for your father to try. Working in the woods alone is asking for trouble. I don't want you to even go near that place."

Tim gave her shoulder a reassuring pat. "Did you forget something, Mom? Dad left our new chain saw and some other gear laying out there where the log fell on him. This is the first chance I've had to go and get it."

Mrs. Bradley looked out at the movement of the bare tree limbs and the leaves that scurried beneath them. "It would be safer to wait until morning. The afternoon wind will blow that little dinghy all around."

"The tide's coming in now," Tim told her. "If I get to the north end of the bay when there's plenty of water, I won't have to follow the channel. I can cut right over the rocks to our landing.

I'll stay all night and come out on the morning tide, so I'd better take my sleeping bag. No food, though. Dad left plenty in the cabin."

The rattling sound came again from the side window as the dog's big nose pressed against the glass.

"Maybe you'd better keep him in the kitchen while I go out the front door," Tim said. "I wouldn't want him following me and trying to crawl into that dinghy."

Tim stepped into the closet near the back door and took his sleeping bag from the top of an open-fronted cabinet which was filled with guns and fishing tackle. He winked at his mother, and stopped to wait in the living room until he heard the back door open. He listened for a moment to the sound of the dog's feet shuffling and padding irregularly in an expression of happiness. Tim eased softly out of the front door, slipped the carrying strap of the sleeping bag over his shoulder, and left the porch in a straight line toward the sea. He walked rapidly through the pasture that lay between the house and the bluff, bracing himself against the wind that shoved jerkily at his left side. A huge boulder, balanced near the edge of the bluff, marked the beginning of a path that angled down the rocky face in sharp switchbacks and ended on a shelf a few feet above the water.

Tim descended, turned off to his right, and followed the shelf to where it curved back from the sea with the face of the cliff. Here, where the cliff receded from the water, the constant washing of the sea had scoured out the softer part of the rocky face to form a cave that opened off the steeply sloping beach.

Back deep in the cave, Tim dropped from the shelf to the sand beside a small white boat. He stowed his sleeping bag in the bow, and turned back to take a small gasoline can from the tools and equipment stored on the shelf. He filled the outboard's gas tank, then stowed the can in the bow. With a grip on the stern, Tim easily slid the boat across the sand until most of it was afloat. He gave a last shove, then landed on one foot, delicately balanced in the tiny craft. While the boat rode on the movement of the water, he tipped the motor into running position and gave the starter rope a pull. The sound of the exhaust rapped loudly against the walls of the stone chamber. Tim throttled down and eased the boat toward the mouth of the cave. Squatting low as he passed under the opening arch, he met the first of the waves with a quick twist of the throttle. The bow raised to meet the lift of the sea, and in half a minute the little boat had shot through the tiny whitecaps and onto the rounded swells. Tim turned north and headed parallel to the coast;

then he slowed the boat to a speed best suited to the seas.

Within five minutes after leaving the cave, Tim headed into the channel that led between the mainland and reef, and into the bay. Nested between the steep shore and the reef, the bay was as quiet as a small inland lake, and within forty minutes the little boat was approaching a low place on the reef near where it joined the peninsula. Here, the top of the reef was so close to the waterline that at this time of high tide the waves on the ocean were visible beyond it. A hundred yards to the left of the low point, a floating dock marked the start of a trail that climbed the heavily timbered slope up to the Bradleys' cabin.

For landing a boat as small as the dinghy, the beach directly ahead was better than the dock. Tim slowed the boat, then as the bow grated on the small stones of the shore, he turned off the motor and tipped it forward. A long, springing step took him over the bow to dry land; then he dragged the dinghy well above the waterline.

As Tim was taking his sleeping bag from the boat, a big wave boomed against the ocean side of the narrow reef and surged across the land and into the quiet waters of the bay as though it were following a channel. Tim dropped his sleeping bag. He ran to where the tongue of the wave had crossed the land, and stared in astonishment. Several waves spent themselves on the ocean side before another slid across the land and into the bay.

Tim glanced at his watch, then studied the little tide pools which showed that the water would come up several feet higher than the level at which the wave had just crossed.

He shook his head in amazement. "An hour from now, that channel will be deep enough to float logs from the ocean to the bay. If I can get logs from our land into the ocean, and then through the reef into the bay, I can get them to the mill." He shook his head again. "Even thinking of it has me talking to myself."

Tim stood motionless, watching one wave after another come nosing through the narrow passage from the ocean to the bay. Finally even the smaller waves surged through, and there was a constant depth of two feet over the highest rocks. There was excitement in his step as Tim picked up his sleeping bag and walked swiftly along the reef past the floating dock to where it joined the mainland.

Five minutes more of steady walking brought Tim into the clearing where he and his father had cut the jack pines to build a snug cabin. He stood for a moment in surprise when he saw that the cabin door was open. The hasp pin, whittled out of pine, hung on a leather thong. He stepped through the door and tossed his sleeping bag onto the bunk.

On the table, an empty bean can sat beside a dirty pan and plate. Tim stepped over to the stove and raised the lid of the coffee pot that stood in its middle, then stared in disgust.

"Boiled dry — grounds and all. Somebody's been here since my dad got hurt. Dad never left a mess like this in his life!"

He walked slowly from the cabin toward where his father had been cutting, studying the ground as he went. When he reached the area where his father had dragged the logs over to a pile, he read the tracks that were visible on the bough-scraped ground. Sometimes the marks of his father's boots were sharp and clear; other times, skid marks and the heavy indentation of the heels told of a man fighting his way backward while leaning hard against the weight of the heavier logs. Tim stood, letting his eyes run over the signs that told how his father had worked at cutting the spruce, trimming out the pulpwood lengths, and then stacking them for fast loading later when there would be enough logs to warrant hiring a tractor and rig to haul them to the mill. His father had been lifting and manhandling logs to the top of the pile when his slippery boot dropped one of his feet between two logs while the weight of another log levered him backward against his jammed leg. At the bottom of the stack was where his father's crawl to the dinghy had started.

Tim shuddered, and turned from the stacked logs to where the freshest trimmings showed that the chain saw had been last used. He scanned the area carefully, then walked over for a closer look. The brows above his green eyes were knitted in bewilderment. "I should be able to see the yellow body on that chain saw against the green of the timber for a quarter of a mile."

Systematically he searched for the saw in a pattern that covered all the ground that had been cut over as well as the space around the log pile and the cabin. At last he quit. "Gone — and it was here when Dad crawled away." He looked at the pile of pulp his father had cut in four days.

"Quite a pile," he said under his breath. "But not enough to start hauling, even if we had money to hire a tractor. And these logs are so far inland that I wouldn't have time to drag them to the water: I'll have to cut my own closer to the shore — even if I have to use the old saw. That means there'll hardly be time even if I *can* get them through the channel and into the bay. I'd better take one more look before I give up on the new saw."

Tim started back over the ground near the cutting area, more slowly this time, and with his head bent low. Next to where the saw should be, there were boot tracks, faint but discernible, leading into and out of the log-scraped clearing. One, plainer than the rest, showed the maker to be a big man. Tim set his foot on the ground near the track and rocked all of his weight back and forth. His shallow print in the moist ground showed that Tim's weight was much less than the maker of the other track. For a long time, as though memorizing the size and shape, he compared the big track with his own. Nightfall made the marks indistinct. With his lean face set in hard lines, he went back to the cabin.

In the cabin, Tim picked a few handfuls of small twigs from the wood box and soon had a fire going in the stove. He took the water bucket from its shelf just inside the door and went to the noisy little stream that tumbled among the trees a short distance behind the cabin. By the time he returned with the water, the back part of the box stove was already cherry-red. He filled the teakettle and set it on the hot spot, then turned to the food shelf.

Whoever had left the mess on the table hadn't taken any other food; there were still several cans on the shelf. Tim took down a can of hash and another of corn. By the time he had opened the cans and set them on the clean end of the table, the teakettle had started to steam. He scoured out the dirty stew pan, then used it as a dishpan for the other dishes. He scrubbed them with strong soap, rinsed them with scalding water, and tipped them over to dry.

The frying pan of hash and the corn in the stew pan were soon ready to eat. While he ate, the wind began to make a shriller sound about the cabin. By the time Tim had finished, the wind was driving a hard downpour of rain against the window. The storm brought darkness early. He lit the lamp that sat in a bracket on the wall, and watched the warm light spread cheerfully over the room.

It was a snug cabin, and like most outdoorsmen Tim relished warm comfort that left him close to the feel of nature and its elements. For a moment, his face relaxed; then it tightened again as he recalled his troubled situation. After Tim had spread his sleeping bag on the bottom bunk, he went over to the window and stood watching the silver and black cords of rain go braiding down the pane. After several thoughtful minutes, he turned, blew out the lamp, and worked his way into the sleeping bag.

He twisted about in a worried way for a short time, and then only the breathing of his heavy sleep and the small noises of the cooling stove were heard.

2

Drops of water in the tops of the trees were sparkling in the morning sunlight when Tim opened his sleeping bag and propped himself up on an elbow. He listened for a few moments, then got up and walked to the window.

"Bright, and no wind. That means quiet water. I can see to wiggle the dinghy out through the rocks without waiting for high tide."

He dressed hurriedly, and stepped from the door of the cabin into the fresh chill of the morning. He closed the door and put the pin deep into the hasp ring, then started swiftly down the slope toward the reef. As he passed the floating landing, he saw that it rode motionless on water that was quiet as a mill pond. When he drew close to the dinghy, he found that the little hull had caught a couple of inches of rainwater. He tipped the boat onto its rail and held it while it drained; then dragged it across the black sand to where low tide had drawn the quiet water. With the bow pointed straight out from shore, he took a shoving step that left him balanced in the little boat.

The motor caught on the third pull, and Tim throttled it down to pick his way slowly among the rocks that protruded several feet above the low tide level. Only a boat as small as the dinghy could clear the rocks that reached at it from the sides and bottom.

"Glad that's over," Tim said as he passed over the last ledge between the shore and the bay's deep water. He opened the throttle until the stern pulled down within a few inches of the quiet water.

In less than half the usual time for such a trip, Tim was pointing the bow toward a black spot that marked the opening of the cave in the bluff. He ducked low as the dinghy passed beneath the archway of the cave. When he cut the engine near the back of the cave, the dinghy was left with enough momentum to push the bow well up onto the smooth sand. He jumped from the boat, and pulled it above the high-tide level; then vaulted up on the ledge and left the cave.

He jumped over the pools the tide had left in the basins at the foot of the cliff, and started up the path that led to the pasture high above.

As he reached the top of the bluff, Tim heard a dog's heavy bark. He looked across the pasture to where the big Newfoundland was moving toward him from the rear of the house. The dog's intense look and stiff-legged walk showed the protectiveness of a watchdog. Suddenly his tail waved in recognition, and he swept across the grass toward Tim. He ran a happy circle around Tim's legs, then sidled his great weight against him and pushed Tim off balance. The dog rooted his big head under Tim's hand.

"Don't figure you've found a home," he said with a gruffness that didn't sound real. "Somebody is bound to come looking for you. And I've got enough problems without worrying about you."

Tide walked at Tim's side until they were almost at the house, then trotted ahead and onto the porch. Mrs. Bradley was standing in the doorway. Tim sniffed at the air that drifted from the kitchen behind her.

"I'll take some of whatever goes with that delicious smell."

"I had just put some bacon on for my breakfast when I saw Tide start across the field. He's been going down to the cave a lot, but when I saw him start out and heard him bark, I thought you might be coming."

Tim gave his mother a quick bear hug, and followed her through the door. "I did my traveling before breakfast, so you can bet I'll be washed and ready by the time you get something on the table."

As is usual with one whose appetite comes from exercise in the woods or on the water, Tim ate in silence. His mother ate a small amount of breakfast, then sat patiently until he finished eating.

Tim looked at her with a glint of excitement in his eyes. "I believe I've found a way to get our logs to the mill without hauling them over the road." He paused to laugh when his mother looked at him incredulously. He got up quickly and went to the old-fashioned kitchen cabinet, returning with a pencil and tablet. He made a hurried sketch of Gull Bay, penciling in the low part of the reef which he had found to be submerged at high tide. "I'll bet nobody's ever been standing there when the tide's full. That little notch must have three feet of water in it for at least four hours a day. And if anybody did see it, he wasn't thinking about floating logs through it into the quiet bay so he could tow them down to the mill. Why should anybody think about it? — we own the shoreline timber. Or we're going to own it."

Mrs. Bradley looked uneasily at Tim. "Your father says you're as good as any man in the woods, but it would take more than one person to get those logs down to the water and started through the reef. I'm proud of you for wanting to try, but it would be too big a job to tackle alone."

Tim's excitement didn't lessen. He rubbed his hands together as though anticipating the job. "If I can get them to the edge of the bluff and start them over, they'll fall into the water."

"What good would it do?" his mother asked. "Even if you could get them to the water and through the reef into the bay, how could you tow them to the mill? Just one jerk on a tow cable would pull our little dinghy apart."

"Then I'll have to get another boat," Tim said.

Mrs. Bradley shook her head. "There's something I must tell you. I've had to borrow money to pay your father's hospital bills. We can't borrow to rent trucks, nor to pay for a boat."

Tim looked down at the big dog lying heavily against his foot. "Boy, you sure brought a long string of bad luck to my family when you got caught on that rock. We needed that job you made me lose."

"Don't let it get you down. You'll find another job," his mother said. "Son," she added, "what about haying? There might be a couple of weeks of that. But you'd better see about it right away."

Tim thought for a few moments before he spoke. "I'm willing to do any kind of work, Mom, but a temporary job won't help us any." He slapped a hand on the edge of the table. "We need to make some real money. And we can make some real money if we can get our logs to the mill. I'm going to try to get a boat." He got up from the table. "I'm going into town now."

"Where will you try?" his mother asked.

"Mr. Gantz is the only one who has the kind of boat I'll need."

"Gantz!" his mother looked at him in disbelief. "You can't mean it. He wouldn't give credit to anyone — especially someone your age. Gantz! Why, with his temper, he would throw you off his place. And with your temper, there'd surely be trouble."

"You can't blame him altogether for his attitude. Some of the fellows have played some low tricks on him. But I was never mixed up in any of it. In fact, I found one of his boats that a couple of characters had towed away and hidden from him."

"He's not apt to remember that," Mrs. Bradley said.

Tim grinned. "Well, I'm off to beard the lion, anyway. If I can't get a boat, I'll promise you I'll see about the haying."

As Tim stood up, the dog walked to the door and waited with his tail wagging expectantly.

"Keep him locked up," Tim said. "I'll need all the good luck I can get — not the kind he brings."

After stepping from the porch, Tim turned and winked cheerfully at his mother, who was hooking the screen door against the probing pressure of

Tide's big nose. "You'd better fasten the other door, too," he called back.

Tim's long, springy gait took him rapidly along the rail-fenced lane to the road. As on the previous day, he walked swiftly and thoughtfully without noting his surroundings. Just before the road became St. Helene's only street, a path, looking like a goat trail, angled crazily down the face of the bluff to a square white building which was fronted by a wharf. The wharf was divided to form a slip from the sea into the front of the building. Several boats rode snugly against the heavy rope bumpers which hung from the wharfsides.

To the left of the boat house, the bluff edged back from the sea to make room for a flat area which was above the waves even at the highest tides. Broken hulls and old boats stripped of parts cluttered most of this space. The steep path ended at a small landing which was propped up on longer legs on the downhill side to compensate for the last few feet of the bluff's slope, so that it formed a level approach to the building's side door.

Above the gentle sounds of the calm sea, the sputtering hiss of acetylene welding was coming through the door as Tim stepped onto the porch. On the far side of the room, which was equipped with a bench and machine tools, Ed Gantz was merging a welding rod and the flame from his torch to run a smooth bead along a crack in the water jacket of an engine block.

Tim turned his eyes away from the torch as the blue light reflected from Ed Gantz's goggles and made eerie colors on the walls and the water of the boat slip that came in through the building's open front. As Tim stepped through the door, there was a rustling sound at his right. A small dog, with a heavily plumed, jaunty tail jumped from a wooden tub that was half full of straw and trotted over to sniff Tim's leg in a friendly fashion. Satisfied, the dog yawned, then went back to his bed in the tub.

Ed Gantz closed the valve on his torch and the flame starved away. Even when he raised his goggles, he gave no sign of seeing Tim. Finally his eyes left the perfect weld he had made, and his head jerked toward the door. "Well, what do you want?"

Tim looked at the heavy frown and tight mouth, and hesitated. "I want to see you, Mr. Gantz."

"You're looking at me," Ed Gantz snapped.

After the light of the welding torch, the room seemed dark, and Gantz's taut face seemed colder and more remote than before. His frown went well up into the skin on his partly bald head. He was of medium height, but his corded arms told that he had the strength and coordination of one who handles heavy objects without help.

"I mean I want to talk to you," Tim went on.

"You're talking now," Ed Gantz said.

Tim clenched his hands and fought to control his voice. "I want to talk to you about getting a boat."

"I've got two to sell — and neither one's cheap." He nodded to a boat that was moored in the slip just below where they were standing. "That one's six hundred."

Tim looked out to the open front of the building where another boat, a heavy-beamed, rugged one, was moored to a buoy. "That's the one I could use."

Gantz looked skeptically at Tim. "Eighteen hundred."

"I want it, but I don't have any money right now."

"Then get out," Gantz said.

Tim didn't move.

"Get out," Gantz repeated.

Tim started to turn, then whirled to face Ed Gantz. His hands were knotted into fists, and he balanced in a way that told he would stay until he was heard. "This is your place, Mr. Gantz, but you're in business, and I've got a right to come here to talk business."

Ed Gantz started across the shop. "Not without money. I'll put you out."

There was a rustling as Gantz's little dog sprang from his tub; then a shrill bark sounded. Tim turned toward the door. He saw the big Newfoundland methodically checking the floor for scent. He raised his head and stiffened as the smaller dog lunged, snapping, against the bigger dog's shoulder.

"Easy, Tide," Tim moved close to the dogs. "He's got a right to sound off when a strange dog comes into his place."

At the sound of Tim's voice, Tide seemed to forget the snapping of the outraged little dog. He shoved hard against Tim, his tail swinging contentedly.

"Don't make any moves toward your dog, and he'll settle down," Tim told Ed Gantz. "Tide knows he's in your dog's place, and he's not apt to hurt him."

"Where did he come from?" Relief softened the man's tone.

"He was caught by a tie rope on a rock in between the harbor and the banks. I went overboard to get him loose. It took time for the crew of the *Cormorant* to stand by and fish us out, so I lost my job."

"Joost?" Gantz asked.

Tim nodded. "That's why I need a boat to make some money."

The hardness returned to the boat builder's face. "The days of making money with a one-man fishing crew are gone."

"I don't want the boat for fishing," Tim told him. "I want it for logging."

Gantz nodded sarcastically. "You want to take *my* boat and try to tow logs through the cross currents and swells outside Long Reef?"

Tim shook his head. "I won't have to go outside. I've found a break in the reef where I can work our logs through and into the bay at high tide. It'll be an easy tow on the bay if I have the right boat — wide-beamed, heavy-keeled, and with a big engine well forward. Like that one over there."

"How did you find out about the tide passage?" Ed Gantz asked.

"I was landing my dinghy on the bay side when I saw waves breaking through. I guess nobody else even knows about it."

"I do," the man said. "I've known for years that you could bring logs through there. But I haven't got any logs, and I didn't see any reason to tell anybody else about it. There's somebody else who's certain to know about it, though. Joost. He's prowled around every bit of that reef."

Gantz looked at the boat moored outside the slip. "How did you figure you could pay for her?"

Tim thought for a moment. "Two hundred a month."

Gantz shook his head. "It would have to be by the week. You could wreck my boat from one month to the next. I'd want to see the boat and get some money every time you sell some logs, and at least one payment each week. If you miss one week, I'm done with you."

"We've got lots of good timber," Tim said, "but I'll be getting it out alone."

Ed Gantz turned and walked back toward his bench.

Tim looked from the man's back to the boat and back again. "I'll take it the way you say, Mr. Gantz. I'll figure out a way to get that timber in, somehow."

"Both tanks are full," the boat builder said. "That's enough for three trips to the notch and back. There's plenty of chain on the wharf heavy enough for pulpwood logs. Take some, and take the comealong and tow cable, too. And that bag of lock links. That's all you need to know. If you can't figure out how to run it, you sure wouldn't be able to tow rafts with it."

With Tide at his heels, Tim went out through the front of the building and across the wharf to the boat mooring. He loaded the chains and comealong-winch, then stood for a moment, studying the boat from the name *Salta* in red letters against the white bow, past the snug-looking cabin, to the heavy stern; then leaned out to place a hand on the rail and vaulted to a spot just behind the engine hatch. In a practiced manner, the big dog jumped and landed just behind him.

Methodically Tim opened the engine hatch door and looked for oil and gas leaks; then pulled the dipstick out to check the oil level. He saw that the boxings that supported the heavy propeller shaft had plenty of grease, and then closed the hatch. He turned one of the gas tank valves on and shoved the transmission level to neutral.

The ignition switch, choke, and starter switch were set on a heavy iron plate which was mounted to the front of the cabin near the wheel and throttle. The engine caught readily, and Tim moved the choke in a bit until it smoothed out and then closed the throttle to idling speed. He hauled on the stern line until the *Salta* was close enough for him to lift the loop from the pile. As his weight rode close to the rail on his way past the engine to free the bowline, he noticed that the boat hardly listed. It was plain that the keel was heavy and deep. With the bowline free, Tim moved quickly back to the controls. He put the transmission in reverse and let the idling engine ease the *Salta* away from her mooring. He smiled as a turn of the wheel changed the heading ninety degrees and sent her boldly out to meet the swells.

Tim held the *Salta* at quarter throttle until she was clear of Gantz's little harbor and then swung her bow up the coast.

"Now's the time to get the feel of her," he told the dog. At all speeds from idling through full throttle he made big and small circles to test the boat's response to the gentle swells. Regardless of the speed or the way she met the seas, the *Salta*'s stability seemed unaffected.

By the time he was off the cave where the dinghy was kept, Tim was able to anticipate the *Salta*'s every reaction to the sea. Now, as he slowed the boat, he stood with one hand on the wheel and the other on the throttle, and laughed at the big dog. Tide was standing up in the bow, feet on the rail, measuring the distance to shore. Every few seconds, he looked back over his shoulder at Tim and swung his tail eagerly.

"You recognize our cave even though you've never seen it from the water before. You've got a sense of direction like a homing pigeon. But we're not putting this big baby in where we keep the dinghy. It goes in what Dad calls 'the slip in our stone pier.' "

From a spot just south of the cove, the "stone pier" jutted out into the bay two hundred feet and then turned to run an equal distance parallel to the shore. On the land side of this parallel, as though built by hand, sharp-sided cuts went straight into the gray rock like the boat slips of a man-made harbor. Tim nosed the *Salta* into the largest of the three slips. Years before, his father and several others had cribbed the closed end and one side of the slip with heavy timbers, and hung them with a variety of salvaged wharf bumpers. He let the idling engine hold the *Salta* against the bumpers while he moved fore and aft quickly to fasten the bow- and stern lines to the rust-encrusted rings on the timbers.

The level of the tide had the *Salta*'s deck riding four feet below the flat stone. Tim hooked his fingers into a crack in the top of a timber and made a jump and pull that brought him where he could get a knee onto the rough surface. He knelt and looked back down at the dog.

"I guess you'll have to hit the water and land on shore."

Tide, standing between the cabin and the rail, confidently gauged the distance up to the pier. He crouched slightly, then with his well-bent stifles driving like springs, he left the deck in a jump that dropped him neatly on the pier in front of Tim.

For several seconds, Tim looked at the dog in astonishment. "How you can fire yourself through the air like that I'll never know — but I'd hate to be in your way. You could knock a man flat. Even a big man, like Joost." He grinned as though enjoying the thought. "Now, let's hurry. Maybe we can get our stuff up to camp, and get in a couple of hours of work before dark."

Tide was already leading the way along the stone pier to the shore. By the time Tim had passed the cave where the dinghy was kept, the dog was nearly to the top of the path up the bluff. He reached the house well ahead of Tim, and his movements on the porch brought Mrs. Bradley to the door. Tim looked at the question on his mother's face.

"Nope — we didn't come back by road, Mom. We came by boat. A good boat. And I'd better be leaving in that boat right away if I'm going to start those logs for the mill. I ought to take a little more food up to the cabin, though. Then in a couple of days, I'll be down with the first logs, and I'll stop by and pick up some more." He stopped to laugh at the look of disbelief on his mother's face. "Really, Mom. We've got a boat."

"From Mr. Gantz? You mean you two hotheads actually talked without losing your tempers?"

"We were both starting to boil over when Tide came tracking me into that boat house. I guess when he saw how Tide held his temper while Mr. Gantz's little dog was chewing on him, we both got ashamed. I'll swear I saw Mr. Gantz smile — probably in relief. He asked me about my dog. When I told him about getting Tide loose from the rock, and having a big run-in with Joost, he started to melt. It was almost as if he had a strong feeling of his own against Joost."

Mrs. Bradley looked gratefully at the dog. "Mr. Gantz seems to have a strong feeling against most other human beings."

"It seemed to be a personal thing," Tim said. "Also — he knows I can get logs through the notch, and he's willing to sell me the boat on weekly payments. That is, he'll be willing until I miss a payment — and that includes this week, which will be over in three days. That means two days to cut the logs, and figure out how to hold them together in a raft, and then tow them to the mill. Let's hope I can collect the money the same day I deliver the logs."

Mrs. Bradley shook her head. "I don't want you to try it alone."

"I've got to. I talked to Mr. Gantz, and I kept my temper. I made an agreement. Now don't make me break it."

Mrs. Bradley began to take food items from the pantry and place them on the table. She used cans kept for that purpose to pack flour and beans. In a much larger can, she packed eggs in yellow cornmeal to protect them from breaking.

The big Newfoundland sat at one end of the table, considerately out of Mrs. Bradley's path, but where he could watch her every move.

"He wonders what you're doing with all that food."

"Part of it's for him," Mrs. Bradley said emphatically. "I'm not going to try to keep him from hunting you down. He might go back to Gantz's boat house and get into trouble."

"I'll take him with me," Tim agreed. He looked at the stack of items on the table. "I'm taking the old chain saw and some other equipment along with this food, so I'll need the wheelbarrow to get it all over to the bluff in one load."

After Tim had left the house, Mrs. Bradley added a half slab of bacon to the supplies, then took a wooden provision box from the pantry and carefully packed the items into it. Tim returned just as she finished, and she held the door open while he carried the supplies out to the wheelbarrow.

When he had finished loading, Tim stood back for one last methodical check. "It looks like there's everything we need to get those logs into the water." He turned to look at the worried expression on his mother's face. Suddenly he hugged her with one arm and mussed up her hair with his free hand. "I'm just going up the bay,

Mom. I'll be back with some loot before Saturday."

"I know you can take care of yourself in the woods," his mother said. "You've been doing it most of your life. But it seems so senseless. Getting those logs out would be a tough, dangerous job for two. How are you going to do it alone? There must be something I can do to help."

"You're doing plenty by taking care of this place," he told her. "The money from our cows and chickens isn't much, but it helps us some."

"But how can you do it alone?" she asked again.

"I don't know yet," Tim admitted. "Dad said to do the best I could. This is the best chance we have, and somehow I'll figure out a way to do it." He picked up the handles of the wheelbarrow and, his green eyes crinkling at the corners, grinned at his mother. "I'll let you know by Friday how I did it."

Tim pushed his load rapidly along the narrow path that cut through the pasture to the bluff. He stopped by the big rock at the point where the path dipped over the bluff's edge, and looked down at the *Salta* riding at the stone pier. "Now for some exercise," he told the dog.

He took the old chain saw from the wheelbarrow and slipped its rope carrying-sling over his shoulder. With the neck of a heavily loaded sack in his left hand and the axe in the other hand, he started down the path. He went swiftly down the steep trail and across the rocks that were still wet from the outgoing tide. He set the load down on the stone pier just above the *Salta* and stretched to work the kinks from his arms and shoulders. He stopped to laugh when he saw the dog measuring the distance down to the boat. "There's another load to bring down before the boat leaves."

The dog looked quizzically at Tim for a moment; then, with sudden understanding, he led the way back to the path and up the bluff. He was sitting knowingly by the wheelbarrow when Tim reached the field.

"I thought you'd figure we were heading back to the house," he said, astonished. "You're making me believe some of those stories about Newfoundlands being mind readers. Who knows? — maybe your talent will pay off sometime."

Tim balanced the box of food on his left shoulder, picked up the remaining sack of supplies, and turned the wheelbarrow over with his toe.

"Now no wind can scoop it over the bluff — but maybe you've already thought about that."

Tide swung his tail agreeably and started back down the path.

When Tim reached the *Salta*'s mooring, he set the box and sack by the other supplies, got a good grip on a piling, and lowered himself into the boat. He watched Tide check for open space and then drop almost straight down, landing poised on the decked-over bow. With one hand keeping a grip on the piling, Tim held the *Salta* against the bumpers while he set the supplies aboard. He held the engine hatch cover open long enough for any fumes to escape, then turned the key and leaned on the starter. The engine, still warm from the run up the bay, smoothed out immediately, and Tim let its idling speed hold the boat against the bumpers while he moved to cast off the bow- and stern lines. He backed out of the slip, and opened the throttle wide as the *Salta* rounded the end of the stone pier and took up a heading for the north end of the bay.

Once the boat was underway, the big dog stood up on the bow deck looking intently across the calm water toward the boundary reef on the north. Occasionally, he turned his head to look at the tree covered bluffs that formed the shores of the bay.

From time to time as the *Salta* eased across the light swells, Tim checked the position of the sun against the landmarks on shore. "It won't be long now, Skipper," he called to the dog. "This hull may not be built for speed, but with our engine and prop, she's twice as fast as the dinghy and outboard."

The shadows from the tall trees on the bluff reached out to darken the rocks and water as the *Salta* approached the small, floating dock that Tim's father had anchored against the reef. While the idling propeller held her against the bumpers, he tied off the lines. He felt only a slight movement of the boat as Tide launched himself onto the dock.

It was no more than a hundred yards from the boat to the camp, but the interior of the cabin was dark by the time Tim had carried the second load of supplies from the boat. He set the last of the things on the floor, and stretched his muscles. He felt his way over to the wall lamp, took a match from the shelf beside it, and in a few moments a mellow light was flooding the room.

"Now we can see to straighten up this mess," he told the dog.

He arranged the foodstuffs in the screened cupboard, and put the saw and other equipment in a corner.

There was plenty of wood for night and morning in the box and enough bark and sticks to kindle it. With skill that showed long experience, Tim arranged the fuel in the stove. Within a few minutes, the little box stove was buffeting the pipe with the force of its draft. He took a bucket from the table and started for the door. Tide watched him step out into the darkness, then trotted out the door after him. When they returned from the creek, the dog resumed his quiet watching from in front of the double bunks.

Tim filled a two-gallon kettle half full of water and set it on the hot spot at the back of the stove, then shook some meat scraps from a paper sack into the water. While the water heated, he removed the spark plug from the chain saw's little engine, cleaned it, and carefully set its gap. He replaced the plug and supplied the engine with oil and fuel from the cans he had brought along. Finally, he set the choke, and gave the starter rope a pull. There was a feeble pop. He shoved the choke in, and pulled again. The sound of the engine's exhaust rapped against the walls, bringing a look of mild curiosity from the dog.

Tim listened approvingly for a bit, then cut the engine and put the saw back in the corner. He stood looking at Tide for a moment. "Lots of dogs would have crawled under the bunk when that racket started. You don't seem to spook very easily."

By the time Tim had washed the grease from his hands, the water in the kettle was boiling. Slowly he shook some of the cornmeal his mother had packed into the water, stirring steadily with a big wooden spoon. When the meal had thickened to a mush, and little geysers of steam were popping through the surface, he slid the kettle to the cool side of the stove.

"When this cools down you'll have a good meal — or several of them. I'll wait until you eat to fix mine. In the meantime, I'll start filing that saw. We'll need everything in our favor if we're going to get a raft of logs to the mill by Friday afternoon."

Tim took the lamp from the wall bracket and placed it on the corner of the table. Now, as he cradled the saw on his legs, he could see to file the best edge on the teeth. He kept moving the blade to bring each tooth into the most convenient position until he had worked his way all around the chain. He put the saw back in the corner and dropped the file into his tool bag.

"It ought to cut wood now," he told the dog.

Tim spooned some of the cornmeal into a big biscuit tin and set it on the table to cool some more. Then he cut six slices of bacon from his slab and put them in the frying pan. When they were nearly fried, he moved them to one side of the pan and cracked four eggs into the hot grease. While they cooked, he put the dog's pan of mush on the floor and set a kettle of water on to heat.

It had been a rough day, and with his hunger deadened by weariness, Tim ate slowly. Tide gave his pan a last lick and lay down before Tim finished eating. The dog watched from his place by the bunks when Tim rose and did up the dishes. He tensed, quick to follow, as Tim took the dishwater outside.

"Take it easy," Tim said as the dog joined him. "I just stopped a minute to check the weather. It looks real good for tomorrow."

He went back into the cabin, sat down on the edge of the bunk, and took off his shoes. "Let's hit the sack so we'll have that saw wound up by the time there's enough light to notch a tree." He pointed a finger at Tide. "And Dog, this time bring me some good luck — I'll need all I can get. What we'll try tomorrow is the only way I can think of to pay my dad's doctor bills and hang onto this timber."

The big Newfoundland rose and walked confidently over and settled his head on Tim's knee.

Tim looked soberly at the dog. "You may have brought me hard luck, but you're sure good company." Suddenly he took his hand off the dog's head. "Let's not forget that somebody will come along looking for you. Anyway, it's time to get some sleep."

He stepped to the table, blew out the lamp, and then eased his way back around the dog and slid into his sleeping bag. As though the darkness and silence in the cabin were a signal, the cry of an owl and other night sounds came from just beyond the cabin walls.

3

Tim awoke when Tide's big nose shoved against the sleeping bag. Though the window showed no lightening of the sky, the first sounds of birds told that dawn was close at hand.

"Good boy," Tim said as he opened the bag. He let the dog out for a run, then felt his way to the matches and lit the lamp. He used small twigs from the wood box to get a quick fire going and cooked a breakfast of oatmeal. While he ate, he could hear the dog moving around outside. By the time he finished washing his pan and dish, it was light enough to make out the dog's form sitting in front of the door. "It's five o'clock and you're ready to go."

Tim left the cabin with the saw, a coil of rope, and the can of gasoline. He walked directly to where his father had started cutting, and then headed toward the stand of trees that grew on the point where the reef joined the mainland. He put his equipment near a jagged stump and with the dog beside him, moved around to carefully study the position of the trees. Satisfied, he walked back to the stump and picked up one of the ropes. When he had fashioned a snug bowline around the dog's neck, he shook about ten feet out of the coil and tied the dog to a piece of the stump. He saw a look of concern on the dog's face.

"Don't worry. I won't leave you. That's just to make sure you're not in the wrong spot when these trees start falling."

The sun had not yet risen when he walked over to a tree and pulled the starter rope on the saw. He made a quick notch in the trunk to direct the fall, and then started another notch a bit higher on the other side. Like most trees used for pulpwood, the spruce was only about ten inches through, and even with the light pressure Tim used to favor the old engine, the tree started swishing downward in less than two minutes. With the inevitable regret felt by an outdoorsman who finds it necessary to cut a living tree, Tim looked at the settling spruce for a moment before moving.

When the fourth tree had fallen, Tim walked slowly down one side of it with the chain saw held at his side, trimming the trunk of branches. He left a few branches near the tip to hold the trunk off the ground, then stepped across the tree and cleaned the other side. Swiftly he trimmed out the other three trees he had cut, then looked over at Tide. "You'll get loose in a minute. While this saw cools, I'll find out what I'll have to do to get those logs in the water. Then I'll know just how heavy those eight-footers can get by the time they're dragged that two hundred yards."

He noticed that Tide paid no attention to his voice, but instead sniffed and pawed at the ground. Tim walked over to the dog and picked up a metal object a bit longer than a lead pencil. "It's only a rusty old saw file," he told the dog. "I don't know why you should be so interested in it, but I guess you're one of those dogs that gets real curious about any odor that's different than the other smells around it."

Tide moved to Tim's side and leaned against him, his tail swinging in a way that showed he appreciated Tim's notice of his ability.

Tim patted the dog's broad head, and put the old file on top of the gas can. "We'll keep it off the ground so you won't have to find it again. Now let's get back to work."

He cut eight-foot lengths from the butt section of each fallen tree and then shut off the saw. Tim untied the dog and while the Newfoundland bounded happily around the area, he threw a timber hitch on one of the logs and made a few overhand knots for handholds a few feet above it.

Tim laid his weight into the rope and felt the

log lift a bit and then move forward. He kept going at a leaning walk until he was close to a point overlooking the head end of the reef. Then he had to lift the butt of the log over the little ledges that protruded from the rock shoulder of the coast. By the time Tim got to the edge of the bluff, he was breathing hard. A hundred feet below and a bit to his right, the reef joined the mainland. He loosened the hitch and rolled the log over the edge. It bounced once off a bulge on the face of the cliff and landed with a loud smack in the ocean close beside the reef.

"Get back," Tim said as the dog crowded the edge. "I didn't throw that in for you to retrieve."

Tim trotted back and threw a hitch on a second log. Even though he had learned the whereabouts of most of the obstructions, he was again breathing heavily when he finally got the second log to the bluff and rolled it over the edge. The third log was a big lighter than the first two and he made the bluff without resting; but when he rolled the eighth one over the bluff, he slumped wearily to the ground and looked down to where the logs were bobbing against the rocks close to the passageway through the reef.

"They're right there ready to be pushed through the notch," he told the dog beside him. "The saw's been working fine, but we'll never make it unless I can figure a way to drag those eight-footers over here faster and without stopping to blow — or unless I can make the day longer. Maybe I can do that. If I get a bunch of logs cut up while it's light, I can keep on dragging them over when it's too dark to saw."

Tim quit talking when he saw the dog stare intently toward a fallen pine that the wind had twisted from its foothold in the soil of the bluff. Though dry, the boughs still held their needles, and hardly visible on a branch near the tip of a tree, a red squirrel had grown bold enough to scold the intruders.

Tide's forehead wrinkled as he trotted over to investigate the sounds. He pushed his way through the tangle of ground-bunched branches to where he had last seen the squirrel on the trunk. As he lunged and floundered through the brushy limbs, they sprang up behind him. Only his head showed above the green tangle. The squirrel streaked out the opposite way on a bare limb and flashed to the ground. Tide tried to back out, only to find that the tough limbs had sprung back into place behind him. When he tried to twist sideways, he found he was boxed in on all sides by the springy branches.

Tired and worried as he was, Tim laughed as the dog, unable to move back or sideways, lunged forward against the trunk of the tree.

The tree slid a bit, and Tide, encouraged by the

small success, humped his powerful rear and shoved again. The tree was only about six inches through and the resilient boughs held the trunk off the ground. Tide continued to shove his great strength forward causing the tip of the tree to sweep in a complete circle around its root end.

Tim laughed again. "I've seen pictures of an ox moving the end of a mill-pole around to grind corn, but I've never seen a dog do anything like it. If you could pull a log like that, you can push — or even help pull. . . ." His voice froze. He stared at the tree that the dog had pushed. It took more strength to move that than to pull the logs he had dragged. Tim shook his head. "We'd need a harness to find out if you'd pull, and we haven't got one. And there's no time to go home for anything wide enough and strong enough to make one out of, so I guess it's back to cutting — even if we haven't figured how to get the logs to the water." He walked back to where he had been cutting, started to pick up the saw, then stopped.

"That reminds me. Dad brought a piece of old belting from the mill saw up here. If I can find it, we might soon have a harness."

With the dog at his side, Tim hurried back to the cabin. Inside, he reached under the lower bunk and pulled a long wooden box out to where he could raise the lid. In neat order, the box held an assortment of things that a woodsman might use to make repairs on equipment, clothing, and shelter. Big washers to be sharpened for axe wedges, rolls of canvas and other cloth for patching, rawhide laces, and a variety of hand tools were a part of the selection. Tightly jammed into a corner was a roll of old belting material. Though softened by hundreds of hours of transmitting power from the pulley of a steam engine to the hub of a mill saw, the belting was practically unbreakable. Around logging camps, material like this had long been a good substitute for such things as shoe soles and hinges.

Tim unrolled the belting on the cabin floor. "Ten feet long and eight inches wide. That's four times what we need."

Tim took a vise from the box and clamped it sideways to the leg of the bunk so that its jaws ran parallel to the floor. He locked one side of the belt's end in its jaws, took a hack-saw from the box and with his left hand gripping the belting opposite the vise, started sawing.

Tide walked over and listened to the sound of the saw on the fabric.

"It's noisy, but it's ten times faster than a knife," Tim told him. "Now, before we cut any farther, I'd better make a pattern with some of these rawhide laces." When he had arranged the laces on the dog and tied them in place, Tim checked the fit, and then removed the pattern so he could use it to measure while he finished cutting the strips of belting. "Now comes the real tailoring part — the slow part — and if you don't make this harness pay off for me, my last chance to win will be gone. Understand?"

Satisfied that the interesting saw noises had stopped, Tide yawned, slumped onto his side and after a couple of contented thumps of his tail, closed his eyes.

"You'd better have more enthusiasm when I put this harness on you or we'll both look silly," Tim said as he turned back to work.

One at a time, he clamped each junction of the strips in the vise according to the rawhide pattern he had made, and then put small holes through both layers with an awl and reamed them out with a file tail so that he could lace them together with the rawhide thongs.

When he had tied the last piece of lace, he called the dog over to him. "Now, stand still while I get this over your head and get this cinch behind your front legs." When the harness was in place, he pulled up and tied the two thongs that tightened the cinch, and stepped back for a look.

Tim snugged up the ties that held the cinch a bit more. "It's a perfect fit, and it won't break. Now, let's go cut a log and see what you can do with it."

As they returned to the timber, Tim called the

dog to him and again tied him away from the dangers of falling trees. The chain saw started on the first pull; Tim notched out a tree and watched it fall as he planned. He trimmed it out, cut an eight-foot length from its butt end, and then went for the dog. He took the rope from the tree and harness and then snugged a timber hitch onto the larger end of the log.

"Now, we've got to figure close, so we both do our pulling at the best angle to the log."

He let the rope slide through his hand while he walked the agreeable Tide out to a position about three feet from the end of the log, then held the line at the dog's back level while he gauged the angle from the log to his hand. Satisfied that the pull would be at the best slope, he tied the rope to the loop on the harness and then cut off the surplus.

"Now you're close enough to cut down the drag, and far enough so the weight won't bear on you when you pull."

Tim picked up the part of the rope which he had cut off and hitched an end of it to the log close to the other hitch.

He was about three feet in front of the dog when he took a handhold on the second rope. "Now, when I pull at this angle, I'll be lifting up on the log a little to keep it from digging in. Let's go."

Tim leaned his weight against the rope and the log started from his pull alone. "Come on, boy," he coaxed.

The log surged forward as the dog's weight tightened the other rope, and then slowed as Tide responded to the feel of the rope as he had when he was tied to the stump. As Tim coaxed and threw his own strength into the rope, the dog moved aside from the log's path and trotted obediently beside it, careful not to tighten his line.

Tim's green eyes squinted, and his jaw was tight with anger as he looked over his shoulder at the dog's position. "You stupid, lazy mutt. I should have left you swimming on the end of that rope instead of fishing you out. You make me lose my job, and then I lose time trying to rig things so you could help me."

Shocked by the scathing tone, the big Newfoundland looked up at Tim for a moment, then lowered his head and shook in shame and confusion.

"It's a good thing I tied you up when I was cutting — you'd be too lazy to get out of the way of a falling tree. Well, I'm not tying you up anymore. You can watch out for yourself. Get on back to where you came from. Just get away from me."

Tim loosened the hitch that held the dog's rope to the log. "What's the use of yelling at you? The time's lost and I'm sunk. But if you tag along, you can at least drag an empty rope while I pull a log. I have to keep trying. I'm caught — just like you were caught when I first saw you."

With disappointment heavy on his face, Tim took his grip on the rope and started the log moving. He didn't look back until he stopped to wipe the sweat from his face and get his breath. He looked dejectedly around and saw that the dog had not moved.

"Tide," he called.

The dog took a tentative step forward, and then looked back at the dragging rope.

"Come on, stupid. You're not anchored," Tim yelled in desperation.

Again the dog took a step, then stopped to look behind him.

Tim let his own rope fall to the ground and walked back toward the dog. Tears came to his eyes as his approach caused the dog to tremble. He knelt down and pulled Tide's head against his chest. "I'm sorry. It's all pretty plain now. As big as you are, you probably broke a few chains and ropes, and they probably got after you for pulling when you're tied. Then I yell at you for doing what you think is right."

The trembling in the big body stopped as Tide rocked his weight from one side to another and shoved his big nose against the side of Tim's head.

Tim gave the dog a pat and rose quickly to his

feet. "Let's try something." He took a long rawhide lace from his pocket and used it to form a noose on the dog's neck. He left about three feet of slack between the dog and his left hand.

"Come on, Tide," Tim said, and started walking without a look back at the dog.

When the rawhide tightened, the dog started, gave one quick look back at the dragging rope, and then trotted along at Tim's left side. Tim stopped and praised the dog until Tide's tail wagged wildly with enthusiasm. Tim gave another command and walked forward. This time, Tide swung into place beside Tim without noticing the drag of the rope. Tim repeated the praise, and then hitched a small tree limb to the rope. Once more the dog started, hesitated for a moment as the rope tightened, and then dragged the limb briskly along in obedience to Tim's tug on the rawhide. Tim stopped and praised the dog until the look of pride on Tide's face left no doubt of his understanding.

"Now, let's give that log another try."

He led the dog back to the log he had cut and again threw a hitch beside that of his own rope. With his rope in his right hand and the rawhide lead in his left, he looked back at the log. "No matter how that rope feels, don't let it make you stop."

Tim stepped forward rapidly in order to start

the log, but before either the rawhide or his rope could tighten, the powerful dog's head was at his side and the log was sliding rapidly along. Tim tried to share the drag of the log by walking faster, but the dog's head stayed even with his side. Once, the log stubbed solidly on a rock, but as soon as Tim turned to pull to one side, the dog matched his move and kept the log sliding. Within three minutes of the time he had started the log, Tide had dragged it to the edge of the bluff.

Tim praised the dog; then he stepped back and looked at Tide, amazed at the tremendous strength he had witnessed. "I was wobbly when I pulled the first one over here, and you're not even breathing hard. I didn't intend for you to pull it all alone. When you get tired and slow down, I can give you some help. Thanks, partner."

Tide turned away from the bluff and trotted ahead of Tim back to the cutting area. Near the spot where Tim's father had dragged logs from the first cutting, the dog stopped and turned his nose questioningly into the soft afternoon breeze. He walked slowly into the cleared spot, reading the air as he went. Tim watched him stop, paw the ground, and then lift a strange object into view.

"What is it this time, you scavenger?" he asked as the dog brought the object to him. "It's an old leather work glove I lost a year ago. It's as dry and stiff as a board. The weather has leached all the oil out of it, and I can't see how there was any smell to it, but I guess that nose of yours told you it was different than anything around it. If it could only help us put logs in the water, but it can't."

He looped his rawhide thong over the jagged stump as a signal for the dog to stay there, and then resumed cutting. Ten more trees fell and were trimmed before Tim stopped the saw. The big dog stood while his rope was hitched to the first eight-foot section of them. Then, as soon as Tim picked up the other rope and rawhide thong, he started the log moving.

Log after log Tide dragged at the speed of a normal walk, without panting, and seemed to need no more rest than he got in trotting back for another hookup.

By noontime the sun was nearly overhead, forty-six trees had been felled, and their logs dragged to the bluff and pushed over to smack the water. Face flushed with excitement, Tim looked down on them. "There's enough there to make the boat payment and have a little left over."

As Tim watched the logs moving around in the wash and the tug of the small waves, he noticed one log align itself with the notch. A wave carried it halfway through the reef before the water became too shallow to bear it. "If something could give that log a little help, it would go on through long before full tide. And if we could get them all through before the water starts to drop, there would be a chance we could get a raft out over the rocks without waiting until tomorrow for the next high tide. Then we'd make it to the mill before quitting time, and Gantz will have his first payment. Should we give it a try?"

The dog shoved his head against Tim's leg, and then followed along back to the piles of tree trimmings. He watched Tim use deft touches of the chain saw to trim one of the discarded tree tops into a clean pole about twelve feet long.

"Now we'll see if my idea will work," Tim said. "But first let's get that rope off you."

With the pole balanced across his shoulder, and a rope in his hand, Tim led the way down the faint trail that ran from the ridge to the reef. As they turned onto the reef and passed the dock, they could see the *Salta* riding the flat water.

"She looks ready to do her job," Tim said as they walked by.

When they reached the notch in the reef, the log which they had watched thread its way into the passage was caught on a shallow hump on the bottom. Tim cut about six feet from his rope and knotted it to the tip of the pole, leaving just enough line to tie a bowline slightly more than a foot in diameter.

The Newfoundland moved up close to the edge of the notch and watched the process with the interest of a water dog. Tim reached out into the passage with his pole, and pushed the log back to deeper water so he could pass the noose over its end. Two full twists of the pole cinched the noose up tight on the log, and Tim started leading it through the channel toward the bay. A bit of lift on the pole started the log over the hump that had stopped it, and then it moved smoothly along. He led it around the big flat rock that stood on the west side of the channel's opening into the bay, and then dragged it onto the small stones of the beach.

He twisted the pole in reverse to free the noose from the log, and walked the few steps back to the ocean side of the reef where another log was nudging the rocks near the opening. He tightened his noose on the log and led it through the channel to a place beside the first.

Within an hour, he had worked all of the logs through the channel to the stony beach of the bay. Tim looked with satisfaction at the spread of logs. "If we can get the bunch worked into a raft and down to the mill, we'll be off to a good start. Now let's get the chains."

With Tide trotting ahead of him, Tim hurried

to the *Salta* and gathered up half of the chains from the deck. He dragged them to a spot near his logs and went back to the boat for the come-along-winch, the rest of the chains and the tow cable.

Tim stretched ten of the chains parallel to each other about two feet apart on the sand. He turned to the logs and started maneuvering them into position across the chains. He selected and added logs until the top ones were about two and a half feet above the sand. Then he began to place logs so that half their length was on that foundation layer and half hung over the end. On the other end, he placed logs in a corresponding position so that the opposing logs met in the middle of the foundation layer. More logs were added until this overhanging layer was two feet above the foundation logs. Tim lifted the chains up over the logs and started to pull them together with the come-along-winch. He tightened each chain repeatedly and held it with a lock-link until the logs were mashed so tightly against each other that the raft was a solid unit.

Tim stepped back and looked with satisfaction at the raft. Compressed by the taut chains it was close to five feet high and equal in width and was a third that size at both ends. The length was a bit less than twenty feet. It was cigar-shaped, similar to the lumber rafts that brought big logs to a lumber mill.

"It looks ready to tow," Tim said. "But it wouldn't be if Ed Gantz hadn't loaned us that winch and lock-links. Ed knows how to do more than build good boats."

He had stopped to stretch his cramped muscles when he noticed the dog staring intently out to the bay. The gentle waves, lifted by the rising tide, had tugged some of the logs from the shore and the breeze was moving them farther out onto the water.

"Six good logs out of reach. It looks like you want to go after them. You'd never get your mouth around them."

Encouraged by Tim's interest, the dog made two plunging jumps that carried him into deep water. He settled low, as powerful strokes pulled him toward the closest log. Tide's natural ability as a true water dog showed when he circled the log and came in behind so that he faced the shore. He found the log's center of balance, and then, with his neck arched over it, started pushing toward the shore.

Tim picked up his pole and was ready when the log came within reach. As he tightened the noose, the dog plunged out toward another log. Tim stood for a moment, admiring the dog's strength and skill, then placed the log near the raft. Without a word of command, or stopping to rest, the dog pushed each of remaining logs within reach; Tim worked high above the water line. "Our raft's finished, so we'll leave them for the next tow."

When the keen-eyed Newfoundland saw no more logs on the bay, he walked to shore, shook himself, and watched Tim make a last check on the raft. Tim hooked one end of a tow cable to the chain on the point of the raft and then, by means of the noose, fastened his pole to the cable's other end; then he flung the pole like a javelin, well out into the bay.

"No!" he shouted as the dog started for the water. "We want the end of that pole to float out there where we can reach it when we move in with the *Salta*. The cable will anchor it from drifting." He dropped a hand on the dog's neck. "Thanks to you, our first logs are ready to go. If we hurry, we can put the tools in the cabin and grab something to eat before the tide's high enough to float the raft."

On the way back to the cabin, Tim picked up the axe, saw, and rope and put them with the comealong inside the cabin. Inside, he poured a panful of water from the bucket for the dog, and then drank two dipperfuls.

"There's no time to build a fire, so we'll each

have a big can of beans and finish the rest of this bread."

They ate hurriedly, and Tim washed the dishes with water from the teakettle which was still slightly warm from the morning fire. The New-foundland was waiting by the door when Tim took a last look around the cabin. Obligingly Tide led the way from the cabin and down the path that led to the reef. From an opening through the tim-ber, Tim saw that the raft was surrounded by water, so they walked faster. The dog ran ahead out onto the reef and past the landing, then dou-bled back and jumped easily to the *Salta*'s deck when he heard Tim's steps on the landing.

Tim gave the engine a routine check and started it. He cast off the lines, then sidled the *Salta* away from the dock and eased her along the reef to a point offshore where the raft lay. Making a turn that put the stern close to the floating pole, he then threw the propeller out of gear. Next Tim pulled the pole from the water until he could get a hold on the cable and remove the rope loop. Finally he fastened the cable's hook to the *Salta*'s tow post, threw the propeller into gear, and let the idling engine tighten the cable.

On shore, the waves were lapping at the high-tide mark. "She'll be floating in a few minutes," Tim told the dog.

Tim studied the different passageways that twisted their courses through the rocks out to the deep water. Plainly it would be impossible to choose a channel for the great length of a boat, cable and raft to thread through. The channel closest to the mainland was the straightest, but it would obviously be shallow.

"We'll take the shallow route," Tim said. "I'd sooner risk bumping the raft on the bottom than hanging it solid on a rock."

He turned again to check the high-tide mark. The waves were now washing over it.

Tim gunned the engine a couple of times to clear it, and then put the prop in gear. He opened the throttle abruptly. The *Salta* came up solid on her cable. He idled the engine so that the cable's weight could pull the boat back. Carefully he studied the pattern of the waves. Just as a swell reached the raft, he opened the throttle again. The *Salta* surged into the cable. The raft caught on the bottom, then slid freely out onto the water of the bay. Tim laughed as the dog, feeling the boat in motion, gave a couple of booming barks. He took the raft well out from shore before he started a gentle turn toward the mainland. Two massive rocks marked the start of the channel he had chosen, and Tim carefully took the *Salta* past that opening; then, as the raft neared the first rock, he doubled back and led the way down the shallow passage. "If we hit bottom, I don't want it to be hard," he said as he slowed the boat.

Tim's tired body tensed and his wool shirt grew damp from the nerve strain as he eased the raft through the channel. Finally the rocks which had flanked the course were behind them and the rocky bottom was far below the sturdy *Salta*'s keel.

"Yahoo!" Tim's wild yell brought the dog spinning around from his eager stance in the bow. He sent two booming barks rolling across the water. As Tim opened the throttle, the big dog turned back to face the direction the *Salta* was headed.

At full throttle, the pull on the cable settled the *Salta*'s stern low in the water. Tim listened exultantly to the steady exhaust, and gave the wheel a pat. "Ed Gantz may be a hotheaded screwball, but he knows his boats." He leaned wearily against the top of the *Salta*'s low cabin, but his green eyes looked triumphantly down the bay.

Without a change in course, the *Salta* dragged her burden down to where the reef closed back toward the mainland to form the bay's narrow mouth; then Tim turned the wheel a bit to take advantage of the deeper water on the mainland side of the opening. When he raised his eyes from his study of the channel, three fishing boats were coming in from his left on a course that would take them south of the pulp mill to the fish cannery. Two of the boats passed as the *Salta* pulled the raft through the bay's opening and headed it across the harbor in the direction of the mill. The last boat drew alongside the *Salta*. It was the *Cormorant*. Joost was standing at the rail, looking down at Tim. Joost was smiling. The smile seemed to fade a bit as the big man faced toward the raft that trailed the smaller boat, then widened as he turned back toward Tim. He raised a huge hand in greeting.

Tim turned to the dog on the bow. "Well, what do you know? He seems positively friendly. It's the first time he's ever smiled at me. I've got a hunch there's a reason for that smile — and another hunch we'll soon find out what that reason is."

4

The two boats stayed abreast until they entered the harbor, then the *Cormorant* headed straight toward the cannery, directly ahead, and Tim turned his boat hard to the right in the direction of the big buildings that housed the pulp mill.

To hold the mass of pulpwood logs that were brought to the mill on bobsleds, when winter snows made such hauling possible, a ring of big timber logs had been chained end to end to encircle a large area of water next to the mill so thousands of the small pulp logs could float close at hand for processing.

Tim shouted to two men who were working on a conveyor that was set to feed pulp logs from the pond into the mill. When the men looked toward him, he folded his arms across his chest then opened them wide in the signal that meant "open for logs."

One of the men picked up a peavey and ran

along the shore to where the ring of fencing logs touched ends. In his caulked boots he trotted confidently along the logs until he reached a place where two of the larger ones were joined by a chain. He dipped his peavey into the water and pulled a short section of the chain to the surface. A hook on the chain of one log joined with the ring on the chain of the other. The man shook the hook from the ring, then put his peavey against the end of the opposite log and shoved heavily.

Tim eased the *Salta* through the opening and took her at idling speed across the quiet water to where a dock stuck out from the front of the mill. The second man had moved from the conveyor to the dock and was standing by to catch Tim's bowline. When the *Salta* was tied off, Tim loosened the tow cable from the stern and handed its end up to the man.

"There's enough cable to reach the shore," Tim said. "We can drag them right up to the beach so I can get my chains off."

By the time they had stepped from the dock to the shore, the man who had opened the passage for the *Salta* was back. The three easily dragged the pulp raft up to where a third of its length was on the beach. The men watched with curiosity as Tim unhooked his chains, and worked them free of the raft.

"There they are, Joe," Tim told the man with

the peavey. "They're all ready to pole onto the conveyor. Now if you'll give me a count on them, maybe I'll be in time to pick up some money."

Joe Vance seemed more interested in the logs than in what Tim was saying. "How'd you get that raft to hold together in the open sea?" he asked.

"I didn't," Tim answered. "I brought them down the bay." He watched astonishment spread over the men's faces. "And I got them into the bay alone. I figure on bringing a lot more down the same way."

"This mill could use a lot of logs in the off-season," Joe said. "Maybe we wouldn't have to lay off part of the crew every year." With a practiced manner, he checked the logs and made notes on a slip of paper which he handed to Tim. "Take this to Grunt Halsey in the office." He turned to look over to where the Newfoundland was nosing at a sand crab. "Did Mr. Hathaway find you?"

Tim looked at Joe curiously. "Mr. Hathaway?"

"The man who owns a dog like that. I thought Joost took him on out to your house."

"Joost? Why would Joost take anyone out to my house?"

Joe shrugged. "It makes sense. Mr. Hathaway came out here asking if anybody in the mill crew had seen his Newfoundland. I guess he hadn't heard about the *Cormorant* pulling a dog out of the water." Joe's pleasant face showed concern as he saw Tim grow tense. "Maybe this is a different dog. I guess there could be more than one of the breed around here."

"It's the same dog," Tim said. "I'm the one who fished him out of the water, and he was pulled aboard the *Cormorant*."

"Anyway," Joe went on, "I told him I'd heard something about a dog on the *Cormorant*, and if he went to the cannery dock he could find out from the captain or Joost where the dog went. Later in the day Mr. Hathaway came back here with Joost. They must have spent a full two hours looking around this mill. You'd a-thought they were figurin' on buying it. They left here together, so it seems that if Joost knew you had the dog, he'd have taken Mr. Hathaway out to your house."

Tim nodded down to the logs at their feet. "I haven't been home all day. I've been cutting those. I'll be bringing in some more within a couple of days. See you then."

Tim stepped up onto the single-plank walk that ran along the front of the mill and with the dog trotting behind, he walked to its far end where a narrow door led into the company's small office. An elderly man, who looked as much a part of the office as its ancient wooden file and the rolltop desk, took two more careful wraps on the salmon fly he was tying and then looked up. He grunted good-naturedly when he saw Tim place the voucher slip on the high counter that divided the room. He grunted again as he read the amount, and then took an old oak cash box from beneath the counter. He counted out a sum of money, then handed Tim a pen and pointed to a line on the slip.

"Thanks," Tim said when he had signed the slip and pushed it back to the man.

"Grunt" Halsey grunted approval and turned his attention back to the salmon fly.

Tim walked swiftly from the office back to the *Salta*. Tide left the office ahead of Tim, jumped down to the sand to chase several scuttling crabs from the shoreline, then bounded up onto the dock and stood watching Tim pick up the chains, cable, and stow them beside his pole on the deck of the *Salta*. He leaped to his place on the bow as Tim started to cast off the lines.

It was only a few minutes from the mill to Gantz's boat house. As Tim sidled the *Salta* up to the dock opposite the gas pump, Ed Gantz appeared at the corner of the building and stepped up onto the dock. Without a word, the man took the nozzle of the gas hose from its hook and handed it to Tim.

"I've got some money for you, Mr. Gantz," Tim said as he took the nozzle.

"I didn't figure you'd come around without it.

If you want any gas, you'd better start filling those tanks."

Tim checked the oil and grease fittings while the tanks filled. "Want to look her over?" he asked.

"Just pay me, and I'll get back to work. You'd better do the same if you want to keep on making those payments."

While Tim counted the money into his hand, Ed Gantz looked at the Newfoundland on the *Salta*'s bow. "You've still got him," he observed. "A man came around here saying he'd lost a Newfoundland."

Tim stiffened as he heard the words. "I haven't seen him."

"Don't give that dog up to anybody but the owner," Gantz said. "You might learn something that way." The boat builder turned from the question on Tim's face and walked rapidly away.

Tim looked from Gantz back to the big Newfoundland on the bow. With each eager movement and mannerism of the dog, the concern on Tim's face deepened. Mechanically he turned his attention to starting the engine. He took the *Salta* sharply away from the dock and heeled her out toward open water. As soon as he was on course, he went to full throttle. His face was set like a wooden mask as he brought the boat into its slip in the stone pier.

When the lines were made fast, Tim ran to shore and headed as fast as he could along the wet, rough footing that led between the tide pools in front of the bluff. His shirt was wet and by the time he had climbed the path up to the pasture, he was gulping the cool air through his open mouth. With his eyes fixed on the ground directly before him, he jogged despondently toward the house.

5

Tim didn't raise his head until Tide barked and bounded toward the house to greet his mother on the porch.

"You're wet from running — is something wrong?" Mrs. Bradley asked.

Tim ignored the question. "Has a man by the name of Hathaway been here?"

"No — but someone else has. Mr. Joost, and with some good news."

"Did Joost mention Mr. Hathaway?"

Mrs. Bradley shook her head. "But let me tell you why he came. He apologized, and said he's going to give you your job back."

"And I'll bet he offered to buy our timberland," Tim cut in.

"Why, yes, he did."

"And I'll bet he said he knows who the owner of the dog is."

"Yes," Mrs. Bradley confirmed.

"But he didn't tell you the man's name. Probably said he'd be real happy to take the dog to him."

"How do you know all that?" Mrs. Bradley asked. "And what's wrong about him feeling sorry that he let you go? Oh — and he actually offered more than we paid for our timber. What's wrong with that?"

"I don't know exactly, but they told me at the mill that Joost and the man with him spent a lot of time looking over the mill and equipment. And that shows Joost is interested in pulpwood. That's why I wasn't surprised at his offer."

"You can tell me what's on your mind while you're eating something," Mrs. Bradley said.

Tim held the door for his mother and Tide, then followed them into the house. "I ate just before I started down with the logs. I'll spend my time talking, and eat when I get back to camp before dark."

"Logs? You mean you did get a raft down here all alone?"

Tim shook his head. "I had help. Lots of it. Let's sit down, and I'll tell you the whole story."

The big Newfoundland lay contentedly on his side while Tim described the tremendous strength the dog had shown in pushing the fallen tree while chasing the squirrel, and how the idea to harness the dog had come about. The dog knew from the frequent glances in his direction that he was the object of attention. Regularly, without moving his head, he rolled his eyes toward the two at the table, and his tail switched against the floor.

"So that's how I happened to be bringing my first raft into the harbor just in time to see Mr. Joost's big smile. That smile made me feel there was a scheme in his mind. If he wasn't scheming about something, he would have brought that Mr. Hathaway along when he came out this morning, instead of coming alone for the dog. He didn't want the man to talk to us. I'm betting the dog is only part of the reason."

"Maybe there's a reasonable explanation. Maybe the man couldn't come along."

"Two things are certain," Tim went on. "Joost wants our timber. And for some reason, he doesn't want this Mr. Hathaway, who says he lost a Newfoundland, to meet us."

"But it was a good offer he made. It would make it easy to pay off your father's doctor bills, and you could go back to school."

"It might look like an easy way, but I've got a hunch it's not the best way. Oh," Tim jumped up from the chair, "I want to look for something in the front yard."

The bare path that led from the porch out to the lane was soft from the previous night's rain. There were sharp footprints in the smooth soil.

"Come out here, Mom," Tim called.

When his mother approached, Tim placed his foot carefully in one of the huge tracks. With his thumb and forefinger he spanned the several inches that the print extended past his toe.

"The man who made this track made the track in the spot where our new chain saw was stolen. I measured it the same way I'm measuring this one, and if Joost made these, then he made those up by the cabin."

Mrs. Bradley stared at the big track. The concern on her face showed she was convinced of what Tim had said. "That may be all the more reason why we should take his offer. If he's so desperate that he'd steal, and even lose face by offering to hire you again, he'll stop at nothing to get what he wants."

A cold look came into Tim's green eyes. "It just might be that Joost isn't as clever as he figures — and maybe I'm not as stupid as he hopes. Dad wouldn't want to sell him our timber, and I don't either."

Mrs. Bradley smiled weakly. "It isn't that I want to sell it. I just can't help tightening up when I think of you out there in the timber alone."

"I keep remembering that you've always told me I could trust the truth to work itself out. And somehow, I never feel alone when I'm out in the woods." He nodded toward the big dog sitting solemnly on the porch. "Now with him along, I feel like I've got a whole crew with me, even if he is just a big, good-natured draft horse."

"He may be strong on the pulling, but I don't know how much protecting he'd do," Mrs. Bradley said.

"Would you protect me, Tide?" Tim asked the dog in mock seriousness.

The great Newfoundland stood up and looked fondly at Tim. His tail swung reassuringly.

"He's certainly big enough to do something," Mrs. Bradley said. "But what about the man who came to town looking for him? You can't very well take the dog along with you now."

"I am," Tim said. "There's some reason why Joost didn't want me to meet that man. And keeping the dog is the one way of being certain that I will meet him. We don't know that the man ever had this dog. Only Joost's word, and that's not much good. If Mr. Hathaway comes around here, you can tell him where I'm at." He looked to where the sun was dipping behind the hills to the west. "If I'm going to get to camp in time to lay in firewood before dark, I'd better get started."

Tim followed his mother back into the house and stood impatiently by the table while she poured him a big glass of milk.

"How are you fixed for food?" she asked.

Tim set the empty milk glass on the table and went through the motions of figuring. "With what you sent along the last time, I should be able to stand a six-month siege." He took the folded money from his pocket where he had placed it after paying Ed Gantz, and laid it on the table. "Here's the rest of the money from our first logs. I made the boat payment, so there's not a lot left. Take what you can to the bank and tell them there'll be more coming in right along. I'll bet that when they see we've actually found a way to get our pulpwood out without a truck or crew, they'll give us an extension on the note. And tell Dad about the logs I sold."

"I'll go in and talk to the bank people on one condition," she said.

"It's a deal," Tim answered. "Now, what is it, Mom?"

"If Mr. Joost is as desperate to get our property as you feel he is, he's going to be wild when I tell him we've turned him down. I probably seemed interested in what he had to say this morning — this was before you brought your raft in, and his offer seemed the only way out of our troubles. He'll feel you're responsible for my change of mind. He knows you'll be working out there alone in the woods, and will probably come out to talk to you. I want you to promise that you won't argue with him or lose your temper — no matter what he says." She placed a hand on Tim's arm. "Promise?"

Tim looked at the lines of worry on his mother's face. He saw a shiver of fright move her shoulders. "I promise. If Joost comes around, I may have to chew on a stick to keep from telling him off, but I'll do my best. Now," he added, "the best way to get Joost out of our hair is to keep those rafts going to the mill. I'll see you tomorrow with some more money. Try not to worry. It's five o'clock and I've got to go now."

Tim left the house with the dog trotting beside him. The smells in the air of the pasture were sharpened by the moisture the rain had left, but the dog did no sniffing about. He stayed at Tim's side as though sharing a mood of thoughtfulness. As they started down the steep bluff to the sea, some gulls were startled from the spray-drenched rocks. Tide ignored their screams. He trotted out onto the stone pier, jumped to his place on the bow of the *Salta*, and stayed sitting quietly while Tim backed the boat out of the slip and headed up the coast for the narrow mouth of the bay.

The *Salta* rode the soft swells of the sea without a noticeable pitch or roll, and the bay was even more quiet, yet Tide pressed flat to the deck of the bow as though he had lost interest. When they reached the floating dock, he jumped from the bow to the dock's rough boards and waited for Tim to snug up the boat's lines.

"They say a dog can tell when there's something worrying his master. But I'm not your master, Old Buddy." He stepped close to the dog and pulled the huge head against his leg. "I guess that may be one of the things bothering me. I keep forgetting you're not mine. Anyway, we don't know that Mr. Hathaway is the one who lost you, so let's both cheer up."

On the way to the cabin, Tim stopped and pulled two limbs from a pile of driftwood that had been trapped in a corner made by the reef and the mainland. They had been crowded to the top of the pile and were dry as kindling. He dragged them up the path to the chopping block in front of the cabin. He got the axe from its place inside the cabin door and quickly broke up the wood to stove lengths. He carried most of what he had cut in to the wood box, then raked up a few handfuls of the wood fragments from around the chopping block and took them in to start a fire in the stove.

The dog stayed close to Tim's side as he went to the creek for water. In the moist ground near the stream, the fresh deep tracks of a heavy buck were still filling with water, but Tide showed no interest in the hot scent.

"That deer scent's so fresh I can almost smell

it myself," Tim said. "I hope you've got more pep than this in the morning when it's time to pull those logs."

Back at the cabin, Tim set the water bucket on its shelf, and took the big kettle from the cupboard.

"There's enough of this cornmeal left from last night to feed you," he told the dog as he spooned the mush and meat scraps into the biscuit tin and set it on the floor.

Tide wagged his tail politely and sniffed at the food. He nibbled at one or two of the meat scraps, then turned from the food and slumped down with a heavy sigh beside the bunk.

"I don't feel like eating, either," Tim told the dog, "but I'd better cram it down if I'm going to wrestle that chain saw tomorrow. While I'm at it, I'll fix enough to warm up for a quick breakfast."

He peeled four big potatoes, put bacon fat in the big frying pan to melt, and then sliced the potatoes into the hot grease. He covered the bottom of a smaller frying pan with a thick slice of ham.

While the food cooked, Tim filled the tank on the saw, and checked the teeth and the tension of the blade. Several times he left the work to get up and stir the potatoes. He noticed that his movements brought no response from Tide. The dog's heavy head remained down on his paws. Even when Tim put the saw back in the corner and washed his hands, the change in activity brought no look of interest from the Newfoundland.

Tim loaded his plate and sat down to eat, then put his fork back on the table.

"Come on over here," he called to the dog.

Obediently Tide came over to the table. "My worries have got you feeling low. Then I see you, and I get to feeling lower. I started it all off, so I guess it's up to me to start us feeling cheerful again."

He reached to the back of the table for another plate. "Now how about having a little of this ham with me?"

He put a few pieces of the meat on the plate and set it in front of the dog.

"Go on — eat it," he encouraged.

More obligingly than hungrily, Tide started to eat.

"Atta boy," Tim approved. "Now wag that old tail."

As the dog's tail moved to the forced gaiety in his voice, Tim's face relaxed for the first time in hours.

"That's the attitude," Tim said. "Let's keep it up."

Tim washed the dishes and put the table and

cupboard in order. As he swept out the cabin, he paused at the door for a look at the sky. Through the gently moving tops of the spruce he could see the stars standing out sharply against the moonless sky.

"It'll be a good morning," he told the dog. "Now that we know what we're doing, we should have those logs going over that bluff like cobs out of a corn sheller. That is, if we get some sleep."

Tim blew out the lamp, then by memory eased his way in the dark around the spot where Tide lay. When he was in his sleeping bag, he hung his arm over the edge of the bunk and let his hand rest on the dog's shoulder. He gave a pat when a sigh moved the dog's heavy body.

"My folks always told me that it helps to believe things will work out all right. This can work out right for us. Maybe tomorrow the man Joost talked to will come around and say he never saw you before. And after that — well, maybe nobody will ever come looking for you again."

6

A few birds were singing when Tide pushed his nose against Tim's shoulder. Tim woke and patted the dog's head.

"You're my favorite alarm clock, but I think you're a bit early."

Tim got up, felt his way across the cabin, and lit the lamp; then he went back to the table and checked his watch.

"It's four-thirty. You hit it just about right," he told the dog. "By the time we get out there, it'll be light enough to see."

He built a fire and dressed while the stove heated; then he ate a quick meal of warmed-over ham and potatoes, and washed up the few dishes.

"Let's get you rigged up," he said to the dog.

Tide stood while the heavy harness was fastened on him, then waited expectantly by the door and watched Tim blow out the lamp and pick up the saw, gas can, and coil of rope. It was light enough to work by the time they got to the cutting area. Tim picked a tree, and then looked for the dog's whereabouts. Motionless in the dim morning light, the dog sat well back from the tree Tim had chosen.

"It looks like you know what this saw means. Maybe you were just cut out to be a timber dog." Tim gave the dog a long, admiring look and then turned his attention back to his work.

As he cut and trimmed tree after tree, Tim took no notice of the passage of time. He was cutting the tip from a springy spruce when the feel of the saw changed; then its motor missed and stopped. He laid the saw on the ground, picked up the coil of rope from where he had dropped it, and called the dog over to him.

"It was running so smoothly, I didn't feel I'd have to stop and cool it; but now it's out of gas, so we'll let it rest a while. Here — hold still." Tim was trying to tie a line on the dog's harness, but Tide kept turning to face down the slope, growling in the direction of the dock.

The sound of a hard-running outboard cut into the silence. The fading of the sound told that a boat was speeding away.

Tim dropped the rope in his hand and streaked down the hill. Near the bottom of the slope, the trees thinned out and he could see the floating dock. The *Salta* was gone. A few more pounding steps brought Tim to within sight of the boat. The

Salta, her starboard side full to the morning breeze, had been blown a hundred yards from shore. She was drifting steadily toward the acres of rocks that lined the bay's channels.

Far down the bay, the outboard motor he had heard was driving a small boat around a shoulder of the mainland. Tim got only a glimpse of the huge man in the stern before the little boat flashed from sight.

Tim pounded onto the planks of the dock, and stood gulping air into his straining lungs. He studied the bend of the shoreline. The land didn't come any closer to the boat than where he stood. He stripped off his boots and outer clothing, then went off the dock in a shallow dive. He surfaced, lined up on the boat, and put all of his strength into a long crawl stroke. For a bit, the distance between Tim and the drifting boat seemed to lessen, then, as his stroke lost its pull, the gap seemed to stay the same. Only a lull in the wind could keep the *Salta* away from the rocks.

Tim looked at the boat, then rolled in the water to check the closest point of land. It was plain from the unevenness in his stroke that there was another problem — his own safety. Close to exhaustion, he needed to be constantly aware of his chances to reach shore in case he began to flounder.

It was at that moment of hesitation when the

great Newfoundland passed on his left side. With the rhythm of a perfect machine, Tide's powerful legs flashed below the surface as they drove the big dog past Tim and toward the *Salta*.

With the dog within calling distance, Tim didn't hesitate to risk his remaining strength in another effort to reach the boat. He could see the dog's speed cut down the distance to the *Salta*. It was plain that Tide's heritage of special breeding had told the dog that Tim was trying to reach the boat.

The distance between the dog's black head and the white boat closed rapidly. He would reach the boat within minutes; but there was no apparent way in which he could hold it off from the rocks.

When Tim again raised his face from the water, the *Salta* was within two boat-lengths of the rocks. He saw Tide swimming alongside the boat toward its bow. Suddenly the dog went even lower in the water as his speed increased. Tide was just past the bow when his neck stretched out and he made a quick grab at something. The dog seemed to be motionless in the water. He had turned back in Tim's direction, but the distance between the dog and boat seemed to remain the same. Then the *Salta*'s bow came around.

The water dripping from Tim's face couldn't hide his look of amazement. He could see that

Tide held the *Salta*'s trailing bowline. The dog's power was bringing her bow into the wind.

Tim's shortened stroke showed his exhaustion. Slowly he pulled his way through the cold water. But now, though he swam at only half his former speed, the distance to the boat lessened. Several times his stroke became only a weak paddling and he sank in the water up to his eyes. Each time, as he seemed about to call to the dog for help, the sight of Tide's grip on the line fired him to a few more weak strokes. He had no more strength to waste on raising his head, and his face was close to the water when he shoved a feebly stroking hand against the *Salta*.

He opened his eyes to the white hull, then prayerfully began to work his way toward the stern where another line might be trailing in the water. Finally he reached a point where he could see the line. He wrapped the stiff fingers of one cold hand around it, and hung with his head just above water. He looked up at the rail, a good three feet above. He filled his aching lungs to their fullest, and sank as far below the surface as his grip would permit. He used the buoyancy of his full lungs and all the strength he could muster to launch himself at the stern rail. At the top of his rise, one outstretched hand smacked the rail and clung. With one hand holding his weight on the rope, he worked the fingers of the other across the rail to a grip on its underside. He took a breath, and pulled his right leg from the water and heaved himself upward and sideways to where he could get his foot over the rail. For several moments he clung with his head swinging loosely with every small movement of the boat; then, with a desperate effort, he rolled himself over the rail and dropped with a thud onto the *Salta*'s deck. He rolled himself over onto his stomach, and then propped himself up on arms that shook with exhaustion. He crawled slowly to the rail and pulled himself close for a look over the side. The dog, with his head turned sideways by the pull of the line in his mouth, was still trying to hold the boat away from the rocks.

Steadier now, Tim looked from the dog to the *Salta*'s control panel, then back again. "I've got to get you on board before I start that propeller," he said under his breath.

Using the rail for support, he moved toward the bow. Tim called several times before the dog appeared to hear him. As Tide stopped pulling, the boat resumed its drift toward the rocks.

"Here, Boy. Drop it and come on!" Tim yelled.

He gripped the rail with one hand and slapped the *Salta*'s side with the other as he walked backward toward the stern. "Drop it. Come on. We don't want to lose her now."

Responding to the urgency in Tim's tone, the Newfoundland released the rope and swam swiftly along the *Salta*'s side to the low rail at the stern. Tim flashed a quick look at the sharp rocks breaking through the blue water on the starboard side; then he gripped the rail above the swimming dog. Tide still had his harness on, but Tim couldn't reach it. He leaned far over and grabbed the scruff of the dog's neck. With the muscles of his jaws knotted and his eyes closed, he heaved himself backward.

Much of the dog's weight was water-borne until the moment when his forepaws touched the rail. It was then that Tim took the full lift. He braced himself and held the dog in position. Tide's great neck raised and stiffened as he reached with one paw, then the other, across the rail. His tremendous shoulder muscles tightened, and the dog came onto the deck.

The closest rocks to the *Salta* were hidden by the rail as Tim lunged to the control panel. He pulled the choke handle, turned the switch, and leaned on the starter. The engine caught, and Tim let it run rough and uneven from the heavy mixture while he spun the wheel to back the boat out into open water.

Away from the rocks, he smoothed the engine, and rested his weight against the panel while the *Salta* traveled back to the floating dock. When the boat nudged against the dock's bumpers, he threw loose hitches with her lines, tightened them, and then started for the cabin. With his first step, he fell forward onto the dock.

7

The floating dock was shielded from the breeze by the spruce-covered slope behind it. The heat of the sun reflected from it, and warmed the air for several feet above the wooden planks. For a half hour Tim lay motionless in the warmth, his head resting on a forearm.

Tide lay close beside him, and several times turned and stretched to touch Tim's arm with his nose. There was more understanding than concern in the dog's expression; and, as though he sensed the time to move was at hand, he stood and pawed lightly with one big foot at Tim's elbow.

Tim opened his eyes and stared dully at the dog. Gradually, comprehension brought focus and reason to his eyes. He moved his mouth several times before words came.

"Thought I'd never make it."

He raised himself on his hands and knees, then crawled over to one of the dock's tie posts and used it for support to pull himself to a standing position. He rocked weakly for a few seconds, then walked slowly off the dock and started up the path that led to the cabin. Some of the color had returned to his face by the time he opened the cabin door. He crossed the room, and sat heavily on the lower bunk. His hand trembled when he held it before him, and he laughed in a light-headed way.

"This weakness is a silly feeling," he told the curious dog. "I need something for energy."

Moving a bit more surely now, he got up and walked to the wood box. There was enough kindling and wood to start a fire, and within a few minutes he had the stove shaking from the draft of burning twigs. After adding a few larger pieces of wood, he then hefted the tea kettle and set it on the back of the stove. He dipped some water from the bucket into a flat pan and set it on the back of the stove. He took a round box of oatmeal from the cupboard and measured two cups of the cereal into the pan, and added a pinch of salt.

"It's not fried chicken, but it cooks in a hurry, and it's got a lot of fuel," he told the dog.

Tim sat on the edge of the bunk until the oatmeal began to steam and pop, then got up to stir it. He spooned the steaming cereal into a soup bowl and covered it with brown sugar. With his big hunting knife, he punched two holes in the top of a milk can and poured its entire contents over the oatmeal. He set tea to brewing, and then sat down to eat.

He ate slowly until most of the food was gone, and drank two cups of the strong tea. After sitting a few minutes, he got stiffly to his feet, and looked at the dog lying beside the bunk.

"If I lay down for five minutes, I wouldn't be back on my feet for five hours. And if we don't have a raft ready to go within four hours, we won't make the tide."

Tim was walking stiffly as he left the cabin, but by the time he reached the cutting area the strength and spring had returned to his step. He stood for a few moments by the chain saw and looked carefully around at the trees he had cut.

He filled the saw's tank from the red gas can, and gave the starter rope a pull. When the engine responded, he revved it a few times and eased the blade against the trunk of a birch. The engine clattered to a stop. Tim pulled the starter rope slowly. There was no resistance from the engine. Tears of frustration brimmed in Tim's eyes. No compression, and that meant a broken valve or a ruined piston. "It can't be fixed." He took no notice of the dog as he walked back to the cabin. Mechanically he drank another cup of tea; then sat staring at the wall. Tide lay on the floor nearby, his head resting on one forepaw.

Finally Tim stood up and spoke to the dog. "It doesn't do any good to say we tried our best. We can't win now. The worst part is telling my dad and mom there's nothing more we can do. I can't think of anything but trying to cut what we can with an axe, and talking Gantz into giving us more time. But I won't blame him if he says no. First, though, we'll get a count on the logs that Dad was racking up when he hurt his leg. Then we'll know how many more we'll have to cut to make a raft."

Tide was still wearing his harness and jumped up eagerly when Tim picked up his axe and left the cabin. While Tim began to count the logs his father had worked into a pile, Tide busied himself with sniffing around on the ground that had been scraped free of cover by the logs they had dragged across it. Several times he came back to center his attention on a spot that appeared no different than the dirt around it. He pawed lightly at the ground, and stopped now and then to hold his nose close to the earth and snuffle noisily.

When Tim turned his attention from counting logs, the dog was digging with both big feet, throwing dirt several feet behind his tail.

Tim looked at the dog impatiently. "Don't be a nose-happy idiot," he said. "There's nothing for you to find on that bare ground. I know you can smell things that are buried, but this is no time to play those games."

The sound of Tim's voice failed to attract Tide's attention. The dirt continued to fly back from his busy feet.

Tim walked over and pulled the dog's harness. "Come on," he snapped, "I said it's no time to play."

Tide braced against Tim's pull. His nose went down to where he had dug, and he grabbed at something.

"You dumbbell," Tim said as the dog pulled a strip of birch bark partway out of the ground. "What's so different about that? There's tons of it all over the place." As Tide gave another tug on the birch bark, Tim bent over the hole and stared at a metal object.

"That's the handle on a chain saw."

Tide moved to one side, tail swinging, and watched Tim lift a chain saw from the shroud of bark in which it had rested.

"It's the new saw that Dad had been cutting with when he got hurt," he said. His face hardened with anger as he stood holding the saw. "Sure — the whole thing makes sense. Joost was so sure of getting our place when he found the saw, he just figured he'd bury it and dig it up later, instead of hauling it away and risk somebody seeing it. It looks like that birch bark kept the dirt away from it, but we'd better go back to the cabin and check it out." For several seconds Tim looked at the big dog. "I'll never again doubt your instinct for sniffing out things that are different from their surroundings. You make it easy to see how good a dog's nose can be. And once again I owe you an apology. Still pals, Tide?"

Tide rooted his nose against Tim's leg, and turned to lead the way to the cabin.

Tim set the saw on the table, and began a careful check of the blade. "Nothing more than the usual dust. It's sharp and the tension's right." He checked the engine's oil level, and the fuel filter. "They're okay, too," he told the inquisitive dog. "Let's go out to the gas can and put a little more fuel in the tank."

The can sat where he'd left it when the old saw broke down. He filled the tank and put the cap back on. "Here goes," he told the dog.

On the fourth pull of the starter rope, the little engine caught. Each time Tim worked the finger throttle, the engine snarled to its full output. He walked over to the tree he'd been cutting when his old saw broke, put the blade against the trunk and opened the throttle. In seconds, the blade ate through the birch.

"Wow — I can see why Dad wanted this saw," he said. "We've still got a good part of the day left, and with this saw maybe we can make up some of the time we lost. We're not licked yet, Tide."

Tide spun around twice and sent a booming bark through the woods.

For three hours, Tim stopped cutting only for fuel and to check the oil level. Then he stopped the saw, and stood breathing heavily as he looked around at the logs he had cut and trimmed.

"That's more than enough to fill out our raft," he told the dog. "Now it's time for you to go to work."

Tide stood while two pull ropes were hitched to a log; then his heavy muscles rippled his shining coat as he started the log forward on Tim's command. Not once did Tim's rope tighten as he picked a way between the cutting area and the bluff. At the edge, he removed the ropes from the log and rolled it over into the water. While he rested a few moments, he looked proudly at the dog.

"With the way you're helping me, I should be able to earn enough money to buy you from that man — that is, if he really owns you. And I guess you'll show whether or not you belong to him when you see him. It's going to take more than Joost's word to convince me that he knows who owns you." Tim smiled at the look of attentiveness on the dog's face. "We've been through a lot together in a few days. How about it — would you like to stay with me?"

The dog sidled over and pushed his head hard against Tim's hip.

For the next two hours Tim and the dog made the trips back and forth from the cutting area to the bluff as fast as they could walk. With each log that he shoved over the edge, Tim could see fewer of the rocks that studded the ocean and bay at low tide. When he had pushed the last of the morning's cutting off into the sea, Tim stood close to the edge and looked down at the narrow reef. Waves were coasting through the notch from ocean to the bay. One log had been nudged completely through the passage into the bay, and two others were floating in the notch.

"We'll be lucky if that tide doesn't drop out from under us before we can get a raft through the rocks."

Tim hurried away from the bluff toward the path that wound down the hill. When he reached the dock, he stepped aboard the *Salta* and took the chains, cable and his pole from their place beside the portside rail and the cabin. He tossed them over the rail, and followed after them to stretch them out on the dock. He threw a hitch onto the chains' hooks with one of the ropes and fastened the rope's other end to Tide's harness.

"I've got a feeling you can handle them easier than I can, as tired as I am."

Tide put his strength against the rope, looked back curiously as the chains clattered on the planks, then followed Tim along the reef to where the marks of yesterday's raft showed in the sand.

Tim laid his pole down while he removed the rope from the chain and harness, then picked the pole up again and went to the notch. He slipped his noose over the end of the first log and tightened it by twisting the pole, then led the log through the channel and onto the beach on the bay side. It was when he had to hold the pole out at arm's length to reach the logs offshore on the ocean side that the strain showed in his face.

"This is no kind of exercise for anybody who's had a long hard swim," he said wearily. "My arms feel like a couple of anchors, and we're not making very good time."

Tim had pulled no more than a dozen logs through the notch and onto the bay's shore when he stopped suddenly and looked at the tide level. He had pulled the first logs onto the sand, just a few inches above the water. Now there was almost a foot of beach between their lower ends and the soft wash of the waves.

"We're too late," he told the dog. "If we try to build a raft far enough out in the water to get it out on a low tide, and don't make it, tonight's high tide would carry it away. Nobody could take a raft out through those rocks after dark, but by the next daylight tide our raft would be gone. There's only one thing to do — drag those logs through and get them above the high-tide level. We'll build the raft in time to catch tomorrow's tide."

As the water dropped lower, and the distance up to the high-tide marks increased, the farther and more difficult the drag up the beach became. Tim turned to the dog questioningly. He called Tide closer to him and tied the rope to his harness. He took his boots off, rolled his pant legs to the knee, and called the dog out to a log he had left bobbing just offshore. He threw a timber hitch on the closest end, and waded ashore. Without a command, the dog dragged the log after him.

When the log had been dragged to a point well above the marks of the highest tides, Tim removed the timber hitch. Suddenly he stopped as though it had just occurred to him how easily the log had been handled. He put his arms around Tide's big neck. "I should call you Lucky Tide.

"It's gotten so natural to depend on you that I do it without even thinking. There's no use fooling myself — I couldn't run this one-man operation without you. But I'll tell you one thing," he went on as the dog's nose rooted against his neck, "with you helping me, I can earn enough money to pay a real stiff price for you. If your owner is willing to sell you. Tomorrow should be the day we'll find out."

Even with the dog helping him, Tim did not finish until the sun had slid behind the trees on the bluff. He took a long look at the logs which were lying in a row well above the high-tide marks, then started for the cabin.

As he was about to pass by the *Salta*, Tim stopped to double-check her tie lines, then stood for a time on the dock and looked appreciatively at the sturdy boat.

"We'd be finished without her," Tim said. "And Joost knows it. He'll try again. Probably tonight. We'd better be ready. That means we'd better go rustle up some grub, so we'll be all squared away by dark."

All through the meal, and while he cleaned up the dishes and table, Tim seemed lost in heavy thought. Dusk was changing the interior of the cabin to indistinct lines and shadows, and he had to feel for the nail as he hung the dishrag on the log wall.

"It's time to get down there," he told the dog, "but it won't hurt to look like we're still in the cabin." He lit the lamp, turned it down low, and set it in the middle of the table.

With his sleeping bag under his arm, Tim

opened the door and quickly followed the dog out into the darkness. Tide seemed puzzled by the unusual time of leaving the cabin and the caution with which Tim picked his way down the path. He stayed within an arm's length of Tim's side.

When they reached the bottom of the slope, Tim put his hand on the dog, and stood for a minute among the thick spruce that fringed the open ground before the dock. He listened carefully, and stared out across the dark water. The dog stood beside him, testing the wind suspiciously. Tim reached over to touch the dog's shoulder, then walked quietly across the rough planks to the *Salta*.

Aboard the boat, Tim opened the narrow door to the cabin. The warmth that had been stored from the day's sun came sweeping out of the companionway. The dog pushed against Tim's leg, and Tim let him lead the way down into the warm blackness of the cabin. The *Salta*'s two bunks were narrow, and there was little room to move between them. Tide stopped at the bunks, and Tim slid by him and dropped the sleeping bag on the portside bunk.

"You might as well nestle down," he told the dog softly. "Here's where we'll spend the night. I should have taken this boat out among the rocks to a hiding place, but it's too dark now. We'll just have to stay awake."

Tim removed only his shoes before he lay down. Though the door was open, it was still warm in the cabin, and he kept the top of the bag turned back. For several hours, restless from the exhaustion and strain of the day, Tim remained wide-awake. As he relaxed in the comfort of the bunk and the warm blackness of the cabin, his periods of tossing grew more infrequent, then quieted altogether, and he lay breathing heavily.

8

Tide was curled on the floor between the ends of the bunks and the door. Tim had been lying quietly for a long time before the dog's head rose, and his body stiffened with several growls. When he stood up, his flank nudged Tim's bunk.

Tim's eyes opened and he stared into the blackness. The dog's growling was making the bunk vibrate against his foot. Tim got to his hands and knees, and reached a hand out to the scruff of the dog's neck. He knelt there, holding Tide firmly for a few minutes, then used his free hand to feel around near the bottom of the sleeping bag. His fingers closed on the cord used for tying the bag. He crawled from the end of the bunk, and tied the sleeping bag cord in a bowline around the dog's neck, then pushed the mattress back so he could tie the cord's other end to the bunk frame.

"I want to get a look at him," he whispered, "before he knows we're here."

With his hand outstretched, he felt his way to

the door and inched up the companionway steps. His eyes, accustomed to the total blackness of the cabin, looked toward the dim outline of the stern rail as he eased along the deck. He went rigid as the *Salta* listed and Tim heard a heavy step near the rail. The hollow sound of the boot on the deck matched another move of the boat. There was the sound of a third step, and suddenly Tim's face bumped into a wool shirt on a burly chest that extended upward higher than his head. He knew it was Joost.

Tim used all of his strength to drive a fist into the body before him, and the man yelled in rage. As Tim jumped backward to avoid the man's rush, his head slapped against the door frame. He crumpled back into the companionway. Trapped by the close sides, there was only one way out. Tim rose to a crouch, pressed hard against the side of the companionway, and plunged as hard as he could up the stairs. One huge hand caught his shirt front, and Tim tried to twist free. The shirt ripped until it reached the double fabric of the shoulders.

Another hand clubbed the side of Tim's head, and he buckled over the two top steps and onto the deck. A hand came from the blackness to grab his left ankle. With all his strength, Tim drove his right foot out and smacked the man's face with his heel. The crushing grip was still on his ankle as he caught the starboard rail and pulled himself up. Tim stood on his right leg, the left one held waist high by the man's hand. Instinctively he leaned backward to avoid a blow, but a big fist crashed against his chest with a force that toppled him back over the rail.

The leverage of his falling weight tore his ankle from the man's grip, and Tim dropped backward into the narrow space between the *Salta* and the dock. He managed to twist sideways so that his head hit the open water between the boat and dock, but his upper right arm slammed against a piling. When he surfaced and tried to swim, the injured arm floated aimlessly in the water. He stopped paddling with his left hand long enough to feel for a handhold on a piling; when his fingers found a notch, he clung desperately.

It was too dark to see another handhold, but he continued to cling to the piling, treading water to take some of the strain from his fingers. Though the lapping of the water against the dock was loud in his ears, he could hear Joost raising the hatch cover. Then a yell of surprise covered all other noises. It was followed by the unmistakable sound of a powerful dog tearing vehemently at an enemy.

Tim's cramped fingers slid from the notch, and he sank into the cold water. As he pawed his way to the surface, a scream of mingled pain and terror came from Joost on deck.

Tim was starting to sink again when he called to the dog for help. With the matchless orientation of a Newfoundland, Tide released his hold, then ran to plunge over the *Salta*'s stern rail. He swam around the stern and into the narrow space between the *Salta* and the dock.

Tim's face was barely above the water when his weak, paddling hand touched the Newfoundland's shoulder. He grabbed the dog's coat and raised himself higher in the water, then made another grab and caught Tide's tail.

The dog's progress was stopped momentarily as Tim's weight sank his rear lower into the water; then the Newfoundland seemed to draw on an amazing reserve of disciplined energy. There was none of the erratic splashing of an ordinary dog as Tide surged through the narrow space along the *Salta*'s side and around the corner of the dock to shore.

The sound of Joost jumping from the *Salta* onto the dock, and running across the planks came from above.

Still holding onto the dog's tail, Tim was half dragged over the rocks to shore. The use of his numbed arm had somewhat returned, and he helped himself over the last of the rocks and up onto the stony beach. Tim knelt for a bit, shivering violently in the chill of the night air, then got to his feet and started up the path to the cabin.

"Thanks again," he told the dog. Suddenly Tim stopped, and leaned against a stump beside the path, while laughter shook his tired body. "I can just see Joost's face when something as black as you are came shooting out of the dark to nail him. I didn't know a man could yell like that. He won't bother the *Salta* anymore tonight — he'll be too busy explaining how he got chewed up."

As they reached the flat in front of the cabin, the sound of a light outboard came from down the bay.

"Hear that? Joost rowed that little boat the last mile or so when he came up here so we wouldn't hear him; but he's probably got only one arm that works now, and he's using the motor."

By the time Tim opened the cabin door, the numbness had left his arm. The flame of the lamp was still burning low as he had left it, and he turned it up bright to flood the cabin with its cheerful light. He scraped up a few handfuls of sticks and chips from the wood box and soon had the little stove pinging from the draft as the dry fuel flared into a hot fire. He removed his wet clothes and hung them on the back of the chair.

His socks, caked with dirt and debris from the path, were tossed against the wall.

Tim rubbed down with a rough towel, and dressed in some of the clothes that his mother had packed in the bottom of the grocery box. Since he had left his shoes down on the *Salta*, Tim fitted himself with one of the three pairs of moccasins that hung beneath the shelf.

"Now let's get something to eat." He looked sharply at the dog. "Come on over here." He took a butcher knife from the table and cut the sleeping bag cord from Tide's neck. "This noose didn't hold you long when you decided to go after Joost." He laughed again. "I can still hear him yelling."

Tim made himself an egg sandwich and a cup of tea and sat down in the warmth of the cabin to enjoy them. He got up to put the pan of leftover oatmeal before the dog, then sat back down to his own meal and watched the dog go hungrily after the pan of food. From the deep strong head, back through the heavily muscled body to the beautifully angulated rear legs, the dog's tremendous power and rare ability were apparent. Tim took a swallow of the hot tea, and grinned.

"I'd like to know what part of Joost you had a hold on," he told Tide. "I guess we'll find out tomorrow."

When Tim had finished his tea, he walked over

to the bunk and pulled the wooden box from beneath it. He opened the lid and took a tightly rolled hudson's bay blanket from its place in the corner. He shoved the box back, and spread the blanket on the bunk.

"It seems like it's been a long enough day. Let's put the lights out."

He blew out the lamp, made his way back to the bunk, and rolled himself in the warmth of the thick blanket. He dropped a hand over the side of the bunk and felt the dog's head slide beneath it. The dog sighed when Tim tugged affectionately at an ear. "It sure makes for good sleeping to have you near. I won't be worrying about Joost any more tonight."

Tim matched another big sigh from the dog with a sigh of his own; then it was very quiet in the cabin.

The stove and table were barely visible in the faint morning light when Tim opened his eyes and looked blinkingly to where Tide was pawing at the hudson's bay blanket.

"Okay — I'll get up. Oh, boy!" he groaned. He nearly dropped down from his propped elbow, but then braced himself, threw back the blanket, and swung his feet out to the floor.

"Those workouts yesterday left me feeling like I'd been playing hockey in a stone quarry." He rubbed the left side of his neck and face gingerly. "That Joost must be part bear. He gave me a few sore spots I'll have for a while. But he sounded more like a rabbit when you had a hold on him."

Tim cooked and ate breakfast in a hurry, but took time to wash his dishes and roll his blanket. He pulled the box from beneath the bunk and stowed the blanket back in place.

As they left the cabin, the dog led the way down the path. He stopped to wait for Tim on the dock.

"We're not ready for our boat ride yet," Tim told him. "I'm just stopping by for my boots."

Tim put a hand on a piling and jumped across the space between the dock and the *Salta*. He froze for a moment as he landed on the deck, then grinned as he picked up a black billfold from near his feet. His grin widened when he opened it. Beneath the transparent cover of one of the packets was a picture of Joost, attached to a mate's license.

"Yipe!" Tim yelled, in a way that made the dog cock his head curiously.

He put the billfold in the chart locker beneath the *Salta*'s wheel, and gave the dog an enthusiastic pat. "We're heading for a big time in town," he said. "It'll be fun watching Mr. Joost's ugly face when he tries to explain why his billfold was found on the *Salta*."

He went down into the *Salta*'s cabin and sat on a bunk while he changed from the moccasins to his boots. Tide was waiting for him when he returned to the deck, and led the way back to the dock and down the beach to the row of logs that he had left strung out just above the tide mark.

He had left the chains lying by the pole just above where he had made the first raft, and he stretched them out a bit closer to the shore.

"We know the way out of here now," he told the dog, "so we can build this thing close enough to the water so it will float before the tide is full."

Though Tim worked slowly because of the soreness in his muscles, the fact that the logs were already on shore made the raft building process go more rapidly. The first waves on the rising tide were just starting to hiss around the bottom logs when Tim hooked the chains on top of the raft. As before, he fastened the noose of his pole to the tow cable and then heaved it hard out into the bay where it popped to the surface as a buoy marking the end of the cable. Tim turned from the water and looked proudly at the raft on the beach.

"It looks like we've done a better job on this one. Now, let's go get the *Salta* and we'll see how it tows."

At the mention of the boat, Tide started for the dock with a stiff-legged gallop generally associated with rocking-horses and enthusiastic puppies. He doubled back several times to check on Tim, part of the time running in the fringe of the water. He reached the *Salta* well ahead of Tim and stood waiting expectantly on the boat.

The engine caught with the first push on the starter, and Tim looked gratefully at the dog on the bow deck.

"It wouldn't be running like that if you hadn't nailed Joost about the time he raised that hatch cover," he mused.

With an idled engine, the *Salta* eased away from the dock and headed down where the pole's end was slanting out of the shining water. Tim backed the boat up and leaned over the stern to grab the pole. He pulled the cable's loop to the surface, freed it from the pole's noose, and fastened it to the boat's post. He nested the pole's heavy end in his right hand, and propelled it in a long arc that dropped it on shore well above the waterline.

He threw the *Salta*'s prop into gear and fed in enough gas to take the slack from the cable. The *Salta* was in deep water when the cable's tautness checked her. Tim opened the throttle and watched the boat's stern pull down from her effort. He waited a few minutes, and tried again. It was on the fourth try that he felt the raft come free.

He began a slow turn that took him angling out from shore to start into the channel he had used for the first trip. It was easier this time to make the turns so that the raft avoided the pattern of rocks, and it was directly in the *Salta*'s wake as she headed down the long, straight channel that led to deep water.

Tim looked at the dog. The boy's expression showed honest pride; he had the confidence that comes with a proven skill. "A few more times through these rocks, and we'll really know this channel. And if we take the bull by the horns — Bull Joost — I've got a hunch we'll keep on making this trip." As he finished talking, he opened the chart locker and gave Joost's billfold a pat.

As the *Salta* and her tow reached the open bay, Tim shoved the throttle forward. More relaxed than he had been for days, he slumped back in the wheelsman's chair and watched the *Salta*'s bow bear down on the narrow mouth of the bay. There were no other boats on the bay, and he saw none on the ocean side of the reef except a few freighters out on the horizon. The shadows of a few big clouds floated like dark, bare islands on the sparkling surface of the water as he cleared the neck of the bay and started the slow turn toward the mill.

He looked out across the smooth water toward the logs that rigged the mill's holding yard and saw that the gate had been left open for him. Joe and his helper were standing on the pier as the *Salta* brought the raft into the holding pond. Joe tied off the boat while the other man stood by for Tim to loosen the tow cable from the stern and pass it up to him. The three of them pulled the raft up onto the shore, and Tim started loosening the chains.

Tide sat watching the work knowingly. As Tim took the count slip from Joe, the big dog turned and bounded toward the catwalk that fronted the building. He ignored the steps, and sprang without effort from the coarse sand of the beach up to the planks; then he turned to look expectantly at Tim.

"I'll bet you guys never saw a dog like him," Tim said. "Look at him—he's only been here once before, and he knows that I'll take this slip to the office. If he does a thing once, he remembers it."

"Oh, I believe it all right. I'd even believe he knows just what to do before it happens," said Joe, who had been looking admiringly at the dog.

"And he's big enough to do it," the helper cut in. "I guess Joost could vouch for that."

Tim's look jerked from the dog and focused in surprise on the man. "What do you mean — Joost?"

The man returned Tim's look of surprise. "Come on now. You didn't think he'd tell the doctor that he got run over by a steamboat, did you? I heard the story from Doc."

"I didn't think he'd want to say anything to anybody about how he got hurt," Tim said.

Both men stared at Tim. Joe finally spoke. "As well as you know Joost, you don't think he'd keep quiet about somebody doing him wrong, do you? Most people were glad to see it happen; but, legally, he's in the right."

"In the right!" Tim repeated in disbelief.

Joe smiled a bit sardonically. "This is about the only time any of us can remember Joost being in the right. It was hard to believe, but he's got the bite to prove it. He still hasn't got my sympathy, though. As ornery as he was in firing you, he deserves a lot of bites."

"Thanks," Tim said. Without another word, he went up the catwalk steps to where the dog was waiting. He followed Tide along the front of the building to the office. As Tim entered the door, Grunt Halsey was sitting in exactly the same position as when Tim had called before. He was tying another salmon fly. With a last pull to tighten a thread, he turned toward Tim.

Grunt Halsey's face showed as much surprise as was possible for one whose features were so heavily creased from years of looking at a ledger. He sat still for a moment before getting up. He grunted three times in crescendo and came over to the counter.

"Didn't expect you back here."

Tim dropped his slip on the counter. "I've got some more logs — why wouldn't I come back?"

The man only grunted in response to Tim's question, then reached for his cash box. He checked the amount on the slip, and counted out some money. While Tim was signing for the payment, the old man leaned around the counter and looked at the dog. "He's the first one I ever knew of to get the best of Joost." With a grunt that could have been either thanks or approval, he put the cash box back in place and took the slip back to his desk.

Tim thanked him, and buttoned the money in his shirt pocket. He followed Tide through the door and back along the catwalk to where his raft lay on the beach.

"The chains and cable are on your boat," Joe called from near the conveyor.

Tim waved his thanks and turned off on the pier to the *Salta*. Tide was settled in his place on the bow by the time Tim started the engine.

"In the right," he said under his breath, repeating Joe's words, as he took the boat away from the pier. "Joost in the right? I wonder what we'll hear next."

When he was out of the holding pond, he opened the throttle. Freed from her burden of logs, the *Salta* responded like a living thing and raised her bow high in the direction of Gantz's boat house. He didn't throttle back until he entered the cove that sheltered Gantz's place. He idled the *Salta* gently against the dock, close to the gas pump. He had tied off and cut the engine when he heard another engine's soft exhaust behind him.

Ed Gantz, in grease-stained coveralls, was hunkered behind the wheel of a stubby workboat that rode low in the water from its load of parts. Without returning Tim's wave, he headed his boat for the opposite side of the dock and the start of the slip that led into the open front of the boat house. He reappeared at the corner of the building, his little dog trotting on stiff legs before him. The small dog's gait became even more stilted when he saw the huge Newfoundland on the *Salta*. He came to the edge of the dock with his weight bouncing from one rigid front leg to the other.

Tide wagged his tail agreeably, yawned, and slumped down on the deck.

The little dog lifted his tail like a flag of victory and, apparently satisfied that the stranger was impressed with his property rights, stalked back to the boat house with dignity.

Ed Gantz looked at the Newfoundland relaxing on the bow. "See you still got him."

"It would be tough getting along without him," Tim answered. "He's kept me ahead of schedule, even though we've had some delays."

"I hear you've been busy with some things beside pulpwood," Ed Gantz said sarcastically. "I heard in town that somebody who says he owns that dog is mad enough to shoot you for making him a biter. And Joost is mad enough to shoot you and the dog — but it looks like his gun arm is out of whack."

Tim's face flooded with red, and the set of his jaw pulled his lips from his teeth. "What's he got to moan about? I'm the one who should do the squawking — and I will."

Ed Gantz studied the angry face before him. "From what I've heard, Joost's in worse shape than you are. But let's hear your side of it — if there is one."

Gantz listened with a look of boredom on his deeply lined face as Tim told of Joost first setting the *Salta* adrift, and then his night attack. Gantz's expression didn't change as Tim pointed out that Tide had twice saved the boat from damage.

The man's silent sarcasm increased Tim's anger. "I'll show you something." He jumped back to the *Salta* and opened the chart closet. He took out the billfold, opened it, and handed it up for Gantz's inspection.

Ed Gantz took the billfold in his work-toughened hand and looked at Joost's license.

"I found it on the deck after the fight. I guess that will show you he was on board the *Salta*. And it'll show the constable, too."

The man handed the billfold back to Tim without comment. "If you want some gas, get that nozzle in a tank. I haven't got time to fool around."

Tim handled the nozzle while Gantz pumped gasoline into the *Salta*'s tanks. When the tanks were full, Tim handed the nozzle back to Gantz. "Would you like to check her over?"

"Not now. I've been lookin' at another boat since yesterday morning," Gantz snapped.

"You mean, all night?" Tim asked.

"Maybe you know somebody who can work on that tub of a *Cormorant* faster. Joost lets things fall apart until they're twice as hard to fix. If it hadn't been for Mower lookin' after that boat, I'd have been there another night."

Tim took the cash from his pocket and counted part of it into Gantz's hand. "We're still ahead on payments — even with Joost trying to mess us up."

"Then why don't you get back to work, and stay ahead?" Gantz asked. "And be smart," he added as Tim turned away. "Put that billfold away and keep it there. Don't say anything about it to the constable. Just stay away from him until he comes after you."

"And act like I'm guilty of something?" Tim protested.

Ed Gantz shrugged his muscular shoulders. "It's up to you. Be smart or be dumb. If you're smart, you'll just keep on working and let Joost make the moves."

Tim watched Ed Gantz walk back toward the boat house as though he were hoping the man would turn and explain something. The little dog trotted out to meet his master and with a happy, sidewinding gait, led the way into the building.

"I guess that's all the talking you'll do today," Tim said in the direction of the man's back.

His face was still flushed with anger as he started the engine and took the *Salta* out of the cove and up the coast.

9

The wind switched to the southeast during the *Salta*'s run to the stone pier. It was snatching the spray from the breakers and tossing it onto the rocks as Tim eased the boat into the slip and tied her off. The soreness in his muscles prompted him to walk around tide pools which he usually jumped over.

The dog was sitting patiently at the top of the bluff when Tim climbed the last few feet of the path. Tim stood for a bit, rubbing the muscles in his thighs.

"I never thought that climb could be so long."

The dog led the way across the pasture, and his sound on the porch brought Mrs. Bradley to the door. Her face was taut with worry, and her hand went to the dog's head in a way that was more of a nervous gesture than a pat. Without a word, she looked at Tim from head to foot. She relaxed somewhat when he smiled.

"Are you hurt?" she asked.

"I've got a sore spot or two," Tim answered. "Why? What makes you ask?"

"Mr. Joost was here this morning — with the constable. He says he was trying to catch and hold you, and you set that big dog on him."

"Catch and hold me! Catch and hold me from *what?*" The red that had come into Tim's face drained, then he whitened from the chill of his rage.

His mother looked at the face before her as though she were seeing it for the first time — a mask of hate that was neither young nor old. "Come on in. I'll fix you some lunch. Then I'll tell you what he said."

"Just tell me," Tim said as he followed her into the kitchen. He stood facing her across the kitchen table as she sat down. "Tell me," he repeated.

"Mr. Joost's wrist was bandaged and in a sling. He says he caught you and was trying to hold you when you called to the dog to come and bite him."

"Caught me? Where?"

"On board the *Cormorant*. He says you were trying to damage his boat when he came aboard and surprised you."

"On board the *Cormorant*. . . . Surprised me. . . ." Tim laughed bitterly. "What did he have to say about a billfold?"

Mrs. Bradley's voice was flat with worry. "He

said you had ransacked his locker and had taken his billfold with his month's wages in it."

Tim fought for control before he started to talk. Then with a reassuring grin he told his mother the facts about his encounter with Joost on the *Salta*, and finding the billfold. "Mr. Gantz must have heard the same thing they told you," he said. "Even about the billfold. Maybe that's why he said to hang onto it until they come after me. What good would it do to go to the constable with my story? There couldn't have been anyone around to see where it happened, so why should they believe me instead of Joost?"

Mrs. Bradley stared at the table without answering. Suddenly she raised her head. "Oh — through all this fuss with Joost and the constable, I forgot to tell you about your father. He can leave the hospital within a couple of days."

"That's one cheerful thing in this whole mess," Tim said.

She shook her head. "It's not that simple. He'll have to keep the cast on for a month. To make it worse, when I went to the bank they told me they can't give us another extension on our loan. They tried to be kind about it, but they said it's impossible for them to grant an extension on the strength of what you can make logging. They would feel secure enough if there were two of you to carry on the operation in case of illness or injury. If your father finds this out, he'll try to work before his leg heals."

"And if there aren't two of us to work, we lose our home." Again there was bitterness in Tim's laugh. "Some choice we've got. But you're right. It's the effect our troubles might have on Dad that's the biggest worry of all."

They were quiet for a while, then Tim smiled. "One thing," he said positively, "we'll still have a roof over our heads, even if it is a small one. It looks like we'll lose our house, but we can always go up and live in the cabin. And I can keep on logging as long as I can hang onto the *Salta*."

Mrs. Bradley looked around fondly at the clean, cheerful kitchen and through the door to where brightly colored rag rugs made the simply furnished living room cozy and bright.

"The three of us have worked a long time to get this little house. It wouldn't bother me too much to go back to living in a cabin, though. But you forgot — you won't be able to work and make the payments on the boat if we don't get this thing with Joost straightened out. He acted very sympathetic to me in front of the constable, and without coming right out and saying so, he let me know our troubles would be over if we sold our timberland to him."

"Our troubles would be just starting, you mean," Tim cut in. "Without our timber there'd be no way to earn money. Even if it paid for the house, we'd have no way of earning a living. We're not selling to him."

"Then you'll have to go in and tell the constable just how Joost came to get his dog bite. It will look like you're guilty if you don't go in and talk to him. This will have to be settled right away."

Tim looked undecidedly at his mother. "It seemed that way to me; then Ed Gantz said I should hang onto that billfold, and not talk to the constable until he came after me. It's hard to tell what's on his mind — it's just like he knows something no one else knows."

"Perhaps he's thinking of himself," Mrs. Bradley said. "If you're arrested, you can't make the payments on the *Salta*, and he'd be released from his bargain. Do you suppose there could be some reason why he'd like to get the *Salta* back?"

Tim shook his head in confusion. For several minutes he stood staring thoughtfully down at the floor. When he raised his head, the indecision was gone from his face. "I can't figure out what he's thinking, or what he could do about any of this, but I'm going back to camp and let the constable come for me. I'm going to trust Ed Gantz."

"I can't advise you not to, because I just don't know what to say."

Tim looked at his mother's worried face for a

few moments, then gave her a cheerful one-armed hug that half carried her toward the door.

"I'll just remind you of what you've always told me, Mom. If we do our very best, nothing can beat us. Now I've got to go. The water was getting choppy, and if I want to get back without being bounced around, I'll have to start." Tim stood for several moments as though trying to think of something more to say, then left the house.

The wind held from the southeast as Tim walked across the pasture to the bluff. He stopped before starting down the path and looked out at the scattered clouds moving swiftly along the horizon. "Maybe along with everything else that's happening we'll get some bad weather to hold us up," he said to the dog beside him.

The tide had fallen, leaving the lowest of the pools draining back into the sea, and the *Salta* noticeably lower at the pier.

As soon as he was out in open water, Tim opened the throttle close to maximum to favor a following sea. The run up the bay to camp was a fast one.

"Hungry?" he asked the dog when the boat had been tied off at the floating dock. "We'll get something going on the stove, and then while it cooks we'll get in a bunch of wood."

He stepped back onto the *Salta* and went below for his sleeping bag. There was no need to spend another night on board; Joost wouldn't try that tactic twice. Back on the dock, Tim turned to recheck the boat's lines, and then started up the path. He picked up a couple of dry limbs on the way to the cabin and dropped them off at the chopping block just outside the door. As soon as he was inside the cabin he built a fire; then he peeled potatoes and put them on to cook. He cut a thick slice of ham and placed it in the skillet to fry slowly on the coolest part of the stove, and then put water on to boil in the dog's mush kettle.

"Now, let's get that firewood."

He dragged several dry limbs to the chopping block and then started cutting them into stove lengths. He interrupted his chopping once to go in and turn the ham, and slowly add the cornmeal to the boiling water, then went right back to swinging the axe. By the time he had carried in the last of what he had chopped, the wood box was full and the food was cooked. He set the kettle of mush on the table to cool, and loaded a plate with ham and potatoes. He ate only a few mouthfuls of food and then stood up from the table.

"I ate breakfast at five this morning — thirteen hours ago — and I'm not hungry. I've heard what worry could do to an appetite, but I never thought it could bother mine. I guess when trouble crowds around close enough and you don't know a way out, you can't forget it for a minute."

He cut up the ham, dumped it on top of the dog's mush, and set the kettle on the floor. "Here, you might as well have it."

The dog sniffed the ham, wagged his tail politely, and moved over to slump down with a heavy sigh by the bunk.

Tim shook his head in a puzzled way. "Now I've got *you* too worried to eat. You sure have a way of knowing that something's wrong even if you don't know what it is."

He washed dishes and put his supplies back in order, then unrolled his sleeping bag on the bunk. "It's too stuffy in here to sleep," he said as he opened the door to the cool night air.

For a long time he lay on top of the sleeping bag, studying the patterns the flickering lamp-light made on the rough lumber of the roof.

"I don't see any way out of this mess," he said to the quiet dog. "Joost has us in a pretty tight squeeze. I'd like to do my best — but how can you do your best when there's nothing you can do but wait? 'Wait for them to come for you,' Ed Gantz said. I guess we're sure to get the answer to that question and a lot of others tomorrow."

It had cooled down in the cabin, and he got up and went to the door. He stood for a few moments listening to the sound of the wind, then closed the door and went back to the bunk and slid his weary body into the snugness of the sleeping bag.

10

It was light when Tim's eyes opened in the morning. He raised his head and looked to where the dog usually stood to paw at his leg and awaken him. Instead, he saw the dog standing rigidly in the center of the cabin, his head moving slightly to each wailing sound the wind was making.

"You're so busy listening to that storm, you forgot to wake me."

Tim slid from the sleeping bag and, as he stood beside the bunk, the floor trembled beneath his feet from the force of the wind wrenching at the cabin.

He stood listening for a moment, then ran to the window. The limbs on the big trees on the cabin's southeast side were bent so far toward their trunks that they appeared to have been cut away. The spruce seedlings which had sprung up in the clearing were whipping against the ground from the force of the gusts. The heaviest of the many broken limbs were rolled and tumbled across the open ground, and lighter fragments were flying through the air, escorted by sheets of rain that moved horizontally like an endless curtain.

"We'd better get down to the *Salta* on the double," Tim said.

He hurried into his clothes and shoved his feet into his boots, making a quick wrap and tie with each lace. He let the dog go out before him, and hung onto the door against the jerking of the wind until he had fastened the latch behind him. He braced against the wind's force and started down the path with his arm held before his face to shield it from the bits of branches that were flying through the air. The dog, his black hair rippling from the wind, moved ahead of him with a crab-like gait. Dead limbs littered the ground all the way to the bottom of the slope. As he drew near the floating dock, Tim could see it tugging at its anchor cables. The *Salta* rode with the structure, snug against her bumpers.

Tim stood on the edge of the dock and studied the play in the boat's mooring lines. He smiled proudly as he looked around at the features that made this spot such a wisely chosen anchorage. Here, the contours of the rocky coastline blocked most of the wind's force except that which was flailing about a few hundred feet away. Each movement of the dock and boat clearly emphasized the advantage of a mooring that could rise and fall with the boat it held. In rough water, a stationary dock would have required enough slack in the *Salta*'s lines to let her drop with the fall of the sea, and each lift of the water would have found her so loosely moored that she would be free to jerk and hammer.

"It took a man like my dad to lay out this place," Tim said with pride. "He's the best outdoorsman in Newfoundland, and there's no reason why he should lose this place or our house."

He looked out across the bay and watched the rain parade in columns across the tumbling surface. "You can't even see the reef," he told the dog. "I don't believe Joost will try to make it up here today. Let's go eat, and dry off."

On the way up the slope to the cabin, fragments of limbs blew against his back. He held the door against the wind while the dog entered, then edged inside and fastened the latch. The thick log walls of the cabin deadened the shriek of the wind to an eerie sound that seemed to come from a great distance.

Tim took a large amount of bark and twigs from the wood box and laid them in the stove. "High wind can bother the draft in a stove," he said as he arranged the fuel carefully. He waited until the tinder was burning hotly before adding larger sticks.

He changed into dry clothes, and hung the wet ones over a chair which he set close to the stove. He took the bacon slab from the cupboard and cut several slices which he put on to fry in the heavy skillet. When he had turned the bacon, he cracked four eggs into the hot grease; they fried quickly and he slid them along with the bacon onto the big plate. He poured the remains of the bacon grease over the mush left in the dog's pan and set it beside the table.

For the first time in several days, Tim ate as though he enjoyed the food.

"You know why I feel like eating?" he asked the dog. "It's the relief in knowing that Joost probably won't be coming around here while this storm holds. I know there'll have to be a show-down, but it's good to know you'll be with me one more day at least."

Tide got up from his place by the bunk, and came over to rest his big head on Tim's knee. He rolled his eyes so that he was looking up at Tim's face.

"Why don't you eat something?"

The dog raised his nose to touch Tim's chest, and then went back to his place at the bunk. Tim watched him lie down and place his head on his forepaws.

"Maybe the wind's bothering you. You don't know that the wind can be a good thing for us."

He looked at the show of wisdom in the dog's dark eyes. "Or maybe you have a way of knowing things that I don't know."

Tim washed his dishes, put the cupboard in order, and then got the new yellow saw from the corner. He took a new file from his toolbox, and started the task of filing and setting the blade's many teeth. When he looked up for a moment to rest his eyes, the dog was watching him soberly.

"My dad told me that a good logger always works on his gear when it's too windy to cut timber. And I guess working on this saw is as good a way as any to show myself that I've got faith that I'll be using it again. I sure wouldn't be showing much faith if I just sat here."

Two hours passed, and Tim had nearly finished work on the saw when Tide got up and started pacing around the cabin, stopping with every few steps, his head cocked to listen attentively.

Tim put down the saw and file, and went to the window. The rain had stopped but the wind was blowing harder.

"You hear the change in the sound of the wind. Maybe it makes you feel like howling."

The shrieking outside the log walls grew higher, and the cabin shuddered from the blasts. Tim turned again to the window. Smaller seedlings growing on the fringe of the clearing were held so flat to the ground that they seemed to have disappeared. Big limbs were riding the wind along with the smaller ones. Tim looked back to the pacing dog.

"It'll be like walking across a battlefield, but we'd better take another look at the *Salta*. She could be fraying her lines."

When he finished tying his bootlaces, Tim closed the damper on the stovepipe and went to the door. Tide went out ahead of him and stood with his black coat and one ear streaming in the wind while Tim locked the door.

There were no lulls in the wind, and with an arm raised as a shield, Tim started across the clearing. He stopped and jumped back as a big branch tumbled erratically before him. By the time he reached the partial shelter where the path started down the timbered slope, he was gasping for breath and tears were standing in his eyes. The going was easier until he hit the level ground before the dock; then, in what was usually a favored area, he broke into the fury of the blast.

He pushed his way into a wind that threatened to hurl him backward until he reached the dock, then he crawled on his hands and knees to the edge to check the *Salta* and her moorings. The boat was riding in the same relationship to the dock, and her lines were snug and sound. He crawled over to one of the piling posts and with its support raised himself to his feet. His fingers dug into the cracks in the rough post, and he looked through tear-blurred eyes at the awesome scene.

Like an invisible trowel, the wind was gouging water away from the rocks until some, which appeared small at even the lowest tides, now loomed monstrously above the surface. Others, never covered by the tides, completely disappeared beneath the water for moments at a time. Outside the reef, on the deep waters of the ocean, mountainous waves rose to completely hide the rock barrier and then fell back to reveal it as a wall topped with a giant fringe of spray. From the reef to the shore, the wind was sweeping the froth from the jagged water and piling it like drifts of snow back among the trees at the bay's edge. The rain had stopped, and the sky was brighter, but the storm became more awesome. The horizon, with its sawtooth edge of waves, was now clearly visible. The only mark on the tapestry of wild water was the black line of a big freighter far to the south.

Tim watched the freighter for a moment, then squinted the tears from his eyes as a smaller black object rose up from the troughs of water on a line with the freighter and less than a mile off the reef. The passing of a cloudbank lightened the sky behind the object and made it stand out sharply. It was a boat.

Tim watched the craft move slowly north until it was about a half mile south of the top of the bay. The boat's progress stopped; she was turning in toward the reef, and her lines were growing distinct. It was the *Cormorant*. She held her course until she was less than a hundred yards off the reef, then put about until her bow was headed back into the seas, and stopped to hold that position. Carefully some of the crewmen lowered a boat and held it while a huge man backed down a rope ladder and skillfully dropped into it. He caught a hold on the bottom of the ladder and steadied the boat while two smaller men boarded it.

With the big man rowing from the middle seat, one of the men in the bow, and the other seated to balance the boat, the dory pulled away from the *Cormorant;* it headed for a low spot in the reef which was buried for the duration of every swell that swept from the ocean to the bay. There were intervals, measured in seconds, when the depth of the swells was enough to let a boat cross the reef. Only a man filled with need or hatred would risk such a small chance. Only men ignorant of the width of the reef would gamble their lives on success. The point toward which the dory headed was separated from Tim by the quarter-mile width of the bay's upper end, and was a half mile to the south.

Several times the tiny dory dropped from sight, each time reappearing a bit closer to the reef. With the bow to the low point, the big man was backstroking to time his try when they dipped from sight again. They reappeared on the face of the next swell. The big man was leaning almost to his back with each mighty stroke of the oars.

Tim knelt and placed a hand on the neck of the dog watching beside him. "They're coming for us," he whispered into a wind that garbled the words on his lips. "I didn't think that even Joost would be in such a hurry for money or revenge that he'd try that — and risk some fools' necks along with his own."

For a time, the mighty strokes of the oars held the little boat to the mountainous face of the swell; then, as it swept across the reef, the peak caught the boat and passed beneath it.

"Oh, no!" Tim's face froze with horror, and his fingers clenched the hair on the dog's neck as the dory dropped from sight. The water slid from the reef, showing the dory with its bow stubbed against a black rock and its stern flush to the sky. Three indistinct shapes lay strewn helplessly on the rocks near it. The foot of the next swell buried the three figures, and sent the broken boat end over end into the bay.

Tim flashed one quick look to the ocean side of the reef where the *Cormorant* was standing by, then reached to the line tied to the piling at his side. In a crouch, he moved to the other piling and loosened the stern line. He straightened partway up, then gave a running jump that landed him on the *Salta*'s deck. The dog landed beside him.

The wind held the *Salta* against her bumpers while he started the engine. He cut the boat sharply away from the dock and started threading a course between the rocks that threatened and retreated with each fall and rise of the water. Tim winced as the *Salta*'s keel sank to nudge a rock which moments before had been deeply buried. As he leaned to stare around the wheelhouse, the wind tore at his eyelids and held the breath from his nose.

When he reached a point opposite the low spot, he closed the throttle and looked toward the reef. Black rocks blocked the *Salta*'s approach to the reef. A seat board, a broken oar, and fragments of wood were flecks on the raging gray water. If anything else of the dory and its occupants remained afloat, it was hidden by the rocks that fenced the *Salta* off from the reef.

Tim closed the throttle and the *Salta* began to wallow aimlessly. He opened the emergency locker near the wheel and jerked a life jacket from the box. He stepped to the rail and tried to throw the jacket, but the wind blew it back over his hand. He let the wind snatch it from him, and he jumped back to the locker. He pulled three round life preservers from the end of the box and forced his way back to the rail. The preservers' wind resistance was slight, and he was able to sail them one at a time out toward the reef.

He stripped off his boots and outer clothing; then he turned his back on the reef and took a careful look toward the beach on the bay's mainland side. One angle seemed to have fewer rocks than the others, and Tim moved quickly to head the idling *Salta*'s bow toward it. When the heading looked right, he locked the wheel and jammed the *Salta*'s throttle half open.

"Let's go!" he yelled to the dog.

With the Newfoundland in the air beside him, Tim dove over the stern rail as the *Salta* lunged across the rock-studded water on the course he had set. His dive, and a few underwater strokes, took him well back among the rocks. He surfaced, shook the water from his face, and turned his head about. Against the black reef, Tim could see the figure of a man clinging to the rocks.

The man used the lift of a wave to work himself higher up onto the steep slope of the rock, clung while the wave fell away, then fought his way above the level of the swells. Once safe, he fell face down on the jagged reef. The water drained from his still form, revealing the uniform of a constable.

Tim turned from the man on the reef and looked around. One of the life preservers was floating close to his hand; two strokes took him to it and with part of his weight bearing on it he could look around him more carefully. In the open space between four big rocks, he saw the dog swimming in a circle, his head raised questioningly above the water. Tim swam toward him and was but a few feet away when the dog headed toward the biggest of the rocks. Tim followed him, and rounded the big rock just as the next swell passed. When the water sank, Tim saw the figure of a man against the face of the rock. It was Joost.

Joost's right arm, with its bandaged hand, was looped over a thin ledge that stuck out from the rock. His weight was tipped toward his left hand which had a finger-hold in a crack. The current was sloping his legs out in front of him against the receding face of the rock.

Tim thrust the life preserver before him and shoved it against Joost's neck. Twice more Tim pushed the life preserver against Joost before the man turned his head. For several seconds Joost stared from eyes that were dulled by exhaustion, then unhooked his arm from the ledge and shoved his bandaged hand through the white circle of the preserver.

Tim raised a hand from the water, pointed in

the direction of the high part of the reef, and then swam away.

The Newfoundland's quartering and circling covered all of the area near the scraps of the boat and took him close to where the swells spilled across the low part of the reef. His circles tightened around one of the smaller rocks and then he stayed behind the rock for a bit. He reappeared, swam a short distance toward Tim, then headed back to the rock.

Wearily Tim inched his way against the currents to the dog. He caught a handhold and pulled himself around to the rock's back side. A man was jammed sideways into a crevice that split the rear of the rock.

At Tim's first glimpse of him, the man's head and shoulders were above water. Tim grabbed the man's collar and held while the next swell came thundering over the reef and buried them. His foot felt the rock beside the man and, as the water fell and lessened the pressure against the still form, he shoved backward.

His pull freed the man and the two of them sank into the water together. By feel, Tim shifted his grip to the man's hair, and fought his way to the surface with frantic strokes of his free arm. The moment his face was clear of the water, he gulped a breath of air, and then started to sink again from the weight of the man.

Tim's head was already below the surface when his wildly flailing hand hit Tide's right flank. His fingers tightened in the hair, and he used his hold on the dog to raise his face above the surface. When the water cleared from his eyes, he shifted his grip to the dog's tail. Tim turned on his back to bring the man's head clear of the surface, and added his own feeble kick to the dog's pull as the Newfoundland dragged him backward through the water.

Through the lift and fall of the swells, the rhythm of Tide's powerful strokes held steadily. Then suddenly the pulling stopped, and Tim's head bumped against the dog. A hand locked onto Tim's wrist, and another hand reached past him to grab the clothing of the man he held. With his eyes turned up at the churning clouds above, Tim was half dragged, half carried up the steep face of the reef, and laid on a flat place close to where the eager dog was standing. When he rolled his head to the right, Tim saw the still form of the stranger being laid beside him. Tide went over and with his brow wrinkled with concern sniffed the unconscious man; then he stood still halfway between the man and Tim.

It was Mower, the *Cormorant*'s second mate, who was kneeling with an ear held close to the mouth of the man who lay so still. "Doesn't sound bad," he said. "This place on his head makes it look like he's more stunned than waterlogged."

"He was dumped and caught on the rocks," Tim said weakly.

"Take it easy," Mower said. "You had a rough time, but we'll all be out on the *Cormorant* in a few minutes."

Tim settled back heavily onto the hardness of the reef. He kept his face turned from the direction in which he had sent the *Salta*, and when Tide watched with interest as Mower lifted and carried the stranger, he closed his eyes. He didn't open them until a hand touched his shoulder.

"It's your turn now," Mower said.

Tim started to get to his feet, then sank back weakly. With help from Mower, he was able to raise himself up and stand.

"Don't walk until you get the feel of the ground," Mower told him.

In a short time, with Mower's support, Tim tried an awkward step. A dozen more steps took him across the reef to the ocean side where a large rubber life raft tilted and righted with the swells. One third of its length had been dragged up onto a shelf of the reef. The constable and Joost were sitting in the seaward end of the raft; the stranger was lying in the center. Crewmen squatted on the reef, bracing sideways as they held to the raft's rope rail.

Tim stepped over the rubber raft's rolled edge and sank down near the stranger. He swayed, and dropped to his side when Mower and the crewmen gave a shove that sent the raft scuffing off the reef and out onto the water.

As awkward as the raft was to row, it was less than a hundred yards to where the *Cormorant* was holding her position, and soon the craft was being held to the fishing boat's port rail. A ladder was put down, and a line was dropped to Mower.

When a running noose had been tied beneath the arms of the unconscious man, he was pulled by the men above and handed up by a man on the ladder until ready hands were able to reach him and lay him on the deck.

Joost rose to his knees and stretched out a big hand to the bottom rung of the ladder. The constable followed close behind Joost.

Mower tapped Tim on the shoulder. "Go on!" he yelled above the sound of the wind.

Tim rolled onto his hands and knees and crawled to the back of the raft. With Mower's help, he raised up to grab the ladder, and hung while the second mate tied a bowline around his chest. With the pull of the line and a shove from below, he was able to make it to the deck.

He tottered away from the rail and sat down to watch while the Newfoundland, slung in a skillfully rigged figure-eight hitch, was hauled over the side. The two crewmen came over the rail followed by Mower, who bent down and shouted something close to the ear of the man at the wheel. As soon as the raft was pulled aboard, the man shoved the throttle forward.

Tim leaned against the side of the ice hatch to steady himself as a surge of power pressed the stern deep into the water. He moved his eyes to follow as Tide walked past to where two crewmen were carefully examining the man lying on the deck.

The man stirred, then moved his head from side to side to look at those beside him. Slowly a look of comprehension came to his face. He looked around more widely, and as he saw the dog his mouth framed a word.

The dog came over to him, and slowly wagged his tail.

The *Cormorant* came straight away from the reef until she was clear of the shallows, then her bow turned toward St. Helene. A man came from below with an armload of blankets and a steaming container that was hung with tin cups. He set the things down near Tim, who was the first one he came to. He tucked one of the blankets around Tim's legs and body, then poured hot tea into one of the big cups.

"You're shakin' and the boat's pitchin', so I just filled it half-full."

Tim opened his eyes and took the cup. He

steadied his elbow on his chest while he sipped the hot liquid.

"This'll hold you till we get into port and dig up some dry clothes for you."

The crewman moved on to where two men had propped the stranger against the port rail, gave them a blanket and some tea for the man, and went on to supply the constable and Joost.

11

Suddenly the hard face of the wind softened, and the men lowered their voices as they talked. The breaks between the clouds widened and the *Cormorant* passed through big patches of warming sunlight.

"Thanks," Tim said as the crewman came over and poured more of the tea into his cup.

There were laughs from several men as the big dog reared to his feet at the sound of Tim's voice, and came over to him.

"Doesn't that make you feel a little ashamed?" the stranger asked as the big dog rested his muzzle on Tim's shoulder. "You could have ruined Tug's character by encouraging him to bite Mr. Joost."

The big Newfoundland turned his head at the sound of his name, looked again to Tim, then moved a few steps away to lie down halfway between the two. Although the boat was going through a sun patch, Tim shivered violently.

"That was a shameful thing for him to bite Mr. Joost." It was Ed Gantz's voice. He was standing near the stern rail, his muscular body turned toward the man in the suit. "Just what night was it that Mr. Joost was attacked?"

"The night before last — Thursday," the man answered in a gentle voice.

Ed Gantz tilted his head with surprise and interest. "Then it was a very quiet thing, wasn't it?"

The stranger studied Gantz's sarcastic expression. "What do you mean?"

Ed Gantz ignored the question. He looked over to where the big mate was huddled in a blanket, then pointed a work-stained finger at the *Cormorant*'s engine hatch. "Joost, what color are the air cleaners on your engines?"

Joost looked sullenly at Ed Gantz. "They're old and greasy. I forget."

"Mower," Gantz called to the second mate, "open those engine hatches."

Everyone on deck looked down at the *Cormorant*'s diesels. In the shadows of the hatches, the new cleaners showed a brilliant red.

Ed Gantz looked at Joost with a sweet patience that was the ultimate in sarcasm. "If you were on this boat Thursday night, you must have seen those cleaners. They're just part of what we put on those engines while we worked all Thursday night. Strange you didn't see them. But then, we didn't see you, either — did we, Mower?"

The second mate studied the sky in a thoughtful manner before answering. "Now that you mention it, I don't remember seeing him on board Thursday night — or Tim and the dog, either."

Every man on the deck heard Mower's words. Every one of them faced Joost. Then they turned to the strange man in the suit, who was staring up at Ed Gantz with the expression of an intelligent man who has been badly fooled.

"Do you mean that Mr. Joost lied about that dog bite?"

Ed Gantz nodded. "Of course. Joost will lie anytime he has something to gain and can find fools to listen to him."

"Here, now," the constable cut in. "Don't you call Mr. Hathaway a fool. He's one of the most successful men in the pulp business. He can do a lot for our area."

"I didn't mean he was as big a fool as you and some others who know Joost, and still believed his story," the boat builder said.

Tim looked at Ed Gantz's face from green eyes that were shining gratefully. Tears of relief almost spilled down his cheeks as he swallowed heavily.

"Why didn't Tim go to the constable with his story?" Mr. Hathaway asked.

"He wanted to tell about Joost coming on board the *Salta* and losing his billfold while he was fighting the dog, but I told him to be quiet about it. It still would have been his word against Mr. Joost's; and with all the fools around, I thought it might pay to let Joost make his story into a formal complaint before we proved we were on the *Cormorant* all night Thursday."

"Mr. Gantz is right," Tim said. "And I'm glad I listened to him."

"I'm glad you did, too," Mr. Hathaway said. "I'd better begin a long apology right now."

"You couldn't help it," Tim said. "It's over now."

Mr. Hathaway shook his head. "No, it isn't. I have a hunch I may have believed some other lies." He paused to nod his head sideways at Mr. Joost. "Did your folks offer to sell him land between his property and the point where the reef joins the mainland?"

"No," Tim said, "but he's been trying to buy it ever since my dad's been in the hospital and we've been needing money badly."

Mr. Hathaway looked scathingly at Joost. "You told me you were buying that property and would lease me rights to move logs across it from any inland timber I might buy." He turned back to Tim. "He said he knew a way to get logs right into the bay."

"My notch in the reef," Tim said. "I've been using it for that."

Mr. Hathaway raised himself unsteadily to his feet with the blanket draped around his shoulders, and then sank back to the deck.

"Sit still a while longer," Mower advised. "You got a good crack on the head when you were jammed in that crevice. You'd be there yet if the dog hadn't led Tim to you."

"Tim?"

"He saved you," Mower said. "And he saved Joost. And just in case you're mixed up on other things, he's the one who first saw your dog in the water the day we found him. Tim had to fight loose from Joost so he could go overboard and save the dog when he was caught by that rope."

The way the man shook his head showed that he had been told a story that was quite different from the truth he was learning from Mower.

"That part about Tug's getting caught by a rope seems to be the only truth that Mr. Joost has told me so far. My little nephew must have tied the rope on the dog's neck. We were all on shore walking around the town when we missed Tug. When he didn't come back, we looked all over for him — on land. The way he swims, we didn't concern ourselves with looking on the water. Now it's plain to see what happened. He just went for a swim and that rope got snagged." He looked thoughtfully at the dog. "He's a little over a year and a half old, and I've never taken time away from business to spend a few hours alone with him. There's no way for him to know that he even belongs to me. And now I find that he's helped to save my life. We should certainly be together more in the future. Right, Tug?"

The dog wagged his tail.

"And it was Tim who saved him," Mower repeated.

Mr. Hathaway sat huddled in his blanket and shook his head from time to time as though trying to adjust his mind to the shock of the truth. The *Cormorant* had entered the quiet water of the harbor when he spoke again.

"My firm has bought a great deal of land from Joost and others," he told Tim. "Bringing our logs across your land and down the bay can save us a lot of time and money. We would pay a nice sum for the lease rights. Would your folks be interested?"

Tim looked happily at the man. "I'm sure they would."

"Good," Mr. Hathaway said. "I'll be out in a couple of days to talk to them. Now," he went on, "there's one more thing. I'll need a man — one with a good cool head, and judgment. You were able to set up an operation alone, so you should be able to — "

Tim stopped the man with a shake of his head, then looked at the Newfoundland lying between them. "I wasn't alone. He pulled every log I cut. I couldn't have done much without him."

"We'll discuss him when I come out to your house," Mr. Hathaway said. "The salary would be good — will you take the job?"

"I can recommend a better man," Tim said. "My dad. He taught me all I know about the woods and water. But I'd like to fill in for a few weeks while his leg heals. Then I'd like to go back to school."

"It will work out," Mr. Hathaway said confidently.

Tim looked to Ed Gantz. "It may take a while, Mr. Gantz, but it looks like we'll be able to pay you for the loss of my boat — your boat."

Ed Gantz snorted. "Loss! What kind of boats do you think I build? You were lucky enough to send her through that bunch of rocks to the only sand on a mile of coast. She's beached high and dry. Tomorrow I'll go in there at high tide and pull her off. I can fix anything that's wrong with her in a couple of days. But you're going to help."

The *Cormorant* slowed, and eased up to the cannery landing. Crewmen stood by with the lines. Tim and the others who were wrapped in blankets got to their feet and stood without difficulty.

The constable and Joost were first off the boat and, with the smaller man talking angrily to the big mate, went rapidly up the cannery steps to the street.

Mower laughed as he watched them go up the steps. "What the constable is saying is just a sample of what Captain Nichols will have to say about Joost taking the *Cormorant* out in that rough water just for his own interests. Joost was gambling that everything would go right for him and he wouldn't need the mate's job anymore."

"You'll make the *Cormorant* a better first mate," Tim said. "The men all like you."

"Enough flattery," Mower said. "How about some dry clothes? We should find something in the cannery."

Mr. Hathaway pointed to a white-and-blue yacht anchored just off a low place in the shoreline several hundred yards north of the cannery. "It's just a few minutes more to my boat — if you can put me aboard."

"We'll use the cannery boat," Mower said. "Now, how about you, Tim? Better dry off before you start that long cool walk."

"I've never felt warmer or better in my life, and the way I feel, I could fly home. Everything seems perfect — " He looked at the dog. "Almost."

"Let's go then," Mower said to Mr. Hathaway,

and started toward a wide-beamed motorboat riding against the landing.

"Let's go aboard, Tug," Mr. Hathaway said, and started after Mower.

The dog followed Mr. Hathaway almost to the boat, then trotted back to where Tim stood.

"I'll help you," Tim said, "but it won't be easy."

He walked across the landing to the boat, and motioned the dog aboard. Mr. Hathaway was already on the boat, and threw his arms around the big dog's neck.

"I understand," he told Tim, "but I'm afraid I feel the same way. I'm sure he'll adjust to staying with me again in a couple of days. If he doesn't, I'll bring him to you when I come to your house Tuesday."

Tim nodded, quickly turned, and headed back to the weathered steps that led up to the street. Echoes sounded in the alley as he went swiftly up the dry, old steps beside the fish conveyor. He turned into the street and walked along, looking straight ahead as though completely occupied with the changes in his life. Occasionally, though, a wistful look came over his face, and he swallowed heavily.

He passed the end of the building, and the motorboat that was taking the dog toward Hathaway's yacht would have been in plain view if he had turned his head a bit. Straight in from the yacht, where the bluff dipped down to let the road come close to the big gray rocks at the shoreline, he stopped and looked out across the water.

Mower was holding the motorboat to the yacht's boarding steps. Mr. Hathaway made his way to the steps and, followed closely by the dog, climbed aboard.

On deck, the dog stood and looked about him with wide, intent moves of his head. Once, his tail swung as though reacting to something the man had said. One turn faced him directly at Tim's still figure on the shore, and he moved closer to the boat's rail. His feet went up onto the rail and he stared intently at Tim for a few moments. Suddenly the dog was in the air.

Tim watched the big body disappear beneath the green water, and he waited for the familiar black head to break the surface. The dog came up swimming on a line that would take him to the rocky beach at Tim's feet.

A voice came across the water and echoed emphatically from the rocks.

"He's your dog now! No use keeping him waiting until I come to your house!" Mr. Hathaway took his cupped hands from his mouth and used one of them to wave cheerily at Tim.

The crest of a wave slapped against a rock and

threw a plume of spray across Tim's face just as Mr. Hathaway turned away.

Tim Bradley used his fingers to wipe away some tears that may have come from the salt of the spray, hunkered wearily and happily against a rock, and waited for Lucky Tide to come to him.

About the Author

WILLIAM R. KOEHLER, chief animal trainer of the Walt Disney Studios for 21 years, is also the author of *The Wonderful World of Disney Animals* and a series of five "Koehler Method" of dog training books. Five of his "pupils," including Asta, Shaggy Dog, and Big Red, have won the conveted Patsy award for outstanding animal performances in motion pictures and television. Mr. Koehler lives in Ontario, California.

APPLE® PAPERBACKS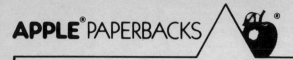

More books you'll love, filled with mystery, adventure, friendship, and fun!

NEW APPLE TITLES

☐ 40388-5   **Cassie Bowen Takes Witch Lessons**
Anna Grossnickle Hines   **$2.50**

☐ 33824-2   **Darci and the Dance Contest**   Martha Tolles   **$2.50**

☐ 40494-6   **The Little Gymnast**   Sheila Haigh   **$2.50**

☐ 40403-2   **A Secret Friend**   Marilyn Sachs   **$2.50**

☐ 40402-4   **The Truth About Mary Rose**   Marilyn Sachs   **$2.50**

☐ 40405-9   **Veronica Ganz**   Marilyn Sachs   **$2.50**

BEST-SELLING APPLE TITLES

☐ 33662-2   **Dede Takes Charge!**   Johanna Hurwitz   **$2.50**

☐ 41042-3   **The Dollhouse Murders**   Betty Ren Wright   **$2.50**

☐ 40755-4   **Ghosts Beneath Our Feet**   Betty Ren Wright   **$2.50**

☐ 40950-6   **The Girl With the Silver Eyes**   Willo Davis Roberts   **$2.50**

☐ 40605-1   **Help! I'm a Prisoner in the Library**   Eth Clifford   **$2.50**

☐ 40724-4   **Katie's Baby-sitting Job**   Martha Tolles   **$2.50**

☐ 40725-2   **Nothing's Fair in Fifth Grade**   Barthe DeClements   **$2.50**

☐ 40382-6   **Oh Honestly, Angela!**   Nancy K. Robinson   **$2.50**

☐ 33894-3   **The Secret of NIMH**   Robert C. O'Brien   **$2.25**

☐ 40180-7   **Sixth Grade Can Really Kill You**   Barthe DeClements   **$2.50**

☐ 40874-7   **Stage Fright**   Ann M. Martin   **$2.50**

☐ 40305-2   **Veronica the Show-off**   Nancy K. Robinson   **$2.50**

☐ 41224-8   **Who's Reading Darci's Diary?**   Martha Tolles   **$2.50**

☐ 41119-5   **Yours Till Niagara Falls, Abby**   Jane O'Connor   **$2.50**

Available wherever you buy books...or use the coupon below.

APPLE® Classics

Exciting adventures that kids everywhere have loved for a long time...so will you!

☐ **40801-1 The Adventures of Huckleberry Finn** by Mark Twain
Troublemaker Huck Finn searches for adventure along the Mississippi River! $2.50

☐ **40800-3 The Adventures of Tom Sawyer** by Mark Twain
Tom and Huck set out on a midnight adventure and wind up witnessing a graveyard murder! $2.50

☐ **40594-2 The Call of the Wild** by Jack London
Buck—part St. Bernard, part German Shepherd—is stolen from his home and treated cruelly. Now he must fight to survive! $2.50

☐ **41293-0 A Christmas Carol** by Charles Dickens
Mean old Scrooge hears the clanking of chains...then a ghost appears! In one terrible hour on Christmas Eve, his life is changed forever. $2.50

☐ **41295-7 Hans Brinker or The Silver Skates** by Mary Mapes Dodge
More than anything, Hans wants to win the big skating race. Does he dare buy new ice skates when they're so poor—and when his father is so mysteriously ill? $2.95

☐ **40719-8 A Little Princess** by Frances Hodgson Burnett
Sara comes to school with a maid, a pony, and lovely dresses. But Miss Minchin makes her live in the bare, freezing attic! $2.95

☐ **40498-9 Little Women** by Louisa May Alcott
You'll never forget the March sisters—Meg, Jo, Beth, and Amy. Share their laughter and their tears. $2.50

☐ **41279-5 Little Men** by Louisa May Alcott
The exciting tale of Jo's school for boys at Plumfield. The sequel to *Little Women*! $2.95

☐ **41269-8 Pollyanna** by Eleanor H. Porter
"You mean I'll never walk again?" Pollyanna has had a terrible accident. Will she ever be happy again? $2.50

☐ **40720-1 The Secret Garden** by Frances Hodgson Burnett
Mary discovers a secret place all her own, in this story of magic and friendship. $2.50

☐ **40523-3 White Fang** by Jack London
He's half dog, half wolf. It's kill or be killed until he finds a master he can trust. But can his master trust White Fang? $2.50

☐ **41294-9 The Wind in the Willows** by Kenneth Grahame
Zany misadventures with Toad and his crazy animal pals, Rat, Mole, and Badger! $2.50

Available wherever you buy books, or use the coupon below.

◀️ Scholastic Inc., P.O. Box 7502, 2932 E. McCarty Street, Jefferson City, MO 65102

Please send me the books I have checked above. I am enclosing $ _____

(please add $1.00 to cover shipping and handling). Send check or money order–no cash or C.O.D.'s please.

Name _____

Address _____

City _____ State/Zip _____

Please allow four to six weeks for delivery. Offer good in U.S.A. only. Sorry, mail order not available to residents of Canada.
Prices subject to change.   AC871